SURVIVORS

DEATH VALLEY

CALIFORNIA, 1849

SURVI

Don't miss any of these survival stories:

TITANIC

FIRE

EARTHQUAKE

BLIZZARD

DEATH VALLEY

And coming soon:

SWAMP

IVORS

DEATH VALLEY:
CALIFORNIA, 1849

KATHLEEN DUEY
and KAREN A. BALE

Aladdin

New York London Toronto Sydney New Delhi

This book is a work of fiction. Any references to historical events, real people, or real places are used fictitiously. Other names, characters, places, and events are products of the author's imagination, and any resemblance to actual events or places or persons, living or dead, is entirely coincidental.

ALADDIN

An imprint of Simon & Schuster Children's Publishing Division

1230 Avenue of the Americas, New York, New York 10020

This Aladdin paperback edition July 2015

Text copyright © 1998 by Kathleen Duey and Karen A. Bale

Cover illustrations copyright © 2015 by David Palumbo

Also available in an Aladdin hardcover edition.

All rights reserved, including the right of reproduction in whole or in part in any form.

ALADDIN is a trademark of Simon & Schuster, Inc., and related logo

is a registered trademark of Simon & Schuster, Inc.

For information about special discounts for bulk purchases, please contact Simon & Schuster Special Sales at 1-866-506-1949 or business@simonandschuster.com.

The Simon & Schuster Speakers Bureau can bring authors to your live event. For more information or to book an event contact the Simon & Schuster Speakers Bureau at 1-866-248-3049 or visit our website at www.simonspeakers.com.

Series design by Jeanine Henderson

Interior designed by Tom Daly

The text of this book was set in Berlin LT Std.

Manufactured in the United States of America 0615 OFF

2 4 6 8 10 9 7 5 3 1

Library of Congress Control Number 98-8422

ISBN 978-1-4814-3127-9 (hc)

ISBN 978-1-4814-3126-2 (pbk)

ISBN 978-1-4814-3128-6 (eBook)

For the women who taught us the meaning of courage:
Erma L. Kosanovich
Katherine B. Bale
Mary E. Peery

SURVIVORS

DEATH VALLEY
CALIFORNIA, 1849

Chapter One

Will was tired. He glanced at his father. How much farther were they going to walk? There was no game here. There hadn't been so much as a rabbit for three days. He shouldered his rifle. "Why don't we just go back to camp, Pa?"

His father turned, tugging his hat brim lower. "Your mother and sister can't go much longer without meat. Nor Eli, nor Jeb."

"Van Patten's brindled ox is about to die, anyway, Pa. Jess told me they're saying they'll still share—"

"I don't like depending on anyone's charity, Will."

Will pressed his lips together to keep from saying what was on his mind. If they had stayed in Illinois, if his father's dreams of California gold hadn't interfered with his good judgment, they would all be sitting around the hearth, stringing popcorn for the Christmas tree. Outside the windows would be snow on the ground, solid and white.

"Over there, Will."

Will followed his father's gesture. There were sparse clumps of sage growing from the rocky soil. As he stared, Will thought he saw the leaves vibrate. Something was crouched between the stalks, hiding. Will felt his mouth water, imagining rabbit stew.

"I'll get around to the side, Will. I'll flush it out toward you."

Will nodded without looking away from the wind-beaten sage. His father's boots ground against the rocky soil. There was no way to move silently here. The howling winter winds had scoured the topsoil, exposing a layer of gravel.

"Watch carefully," Will's father said quietly. "If it makes a run back this way, call out. Maybe I can get a shot at it."

Will glanced up, then his eyes returned to the sage. His father walked closer, as intent as any mountain lion, knees bent, his rifle half raised. Will said a little prayer and raised his own rifle. They had almost used up the bags of flour and rice they'd bought from the

Mormon storekeep in the new little settlement on Salt Lake.

Will held the rifle steady, breathing evenly, waiting. Without meaning to, he pictured their old kitchen table, the one they'd left beside the trail a few weeks out of Fort Laramie the first time they had had to lighten the wagon. It felt like their lives were scattered behind them all the way back to Illinois. Most of their furniture was gone; they had traded his mother's trunk for new iron tires on the wagon wheels.

Will glanced at his father—he was slowly advancing on the clump of sage. Will allowed himself to think about what a real supper would be like. He could see it so clearly, smell the inviting scents of his mother's chicken and dumplings, her fruit pies, steamed sweet corn and yams. His mouth flooded with saliva again.

"Will!"

He jerked his head up to look at his father.

"Is it still in there? Did you see it run?"

Will shook his head, pretty sure he hadn't actually closed his eyes. He was so tired. They hadn't had enough water for days—or enough food, really, even though the families were sharing meat whenever anyone had to kill one of the oxen.

The sage shook suddenly, and Will pulled the hammer all the way back, waiting tensely. Then he settled the rifle snug into his shoulder and aimed at the blur of motion that burst clear a second later. Steady, deliberate, he pulled the trigger.

"You got him! He's a big one," Will's father called, holding the rabbit up by one hind leg.

Will smiled, tapping powder into his rifle. He rammed the shot home, then slid the rod back into its scabbard, reaching for the pouch that held his percussion caps.

Following his father's impatient gesture, he began to wade through the scrubby line of sage where the rabbit had hidden. There was a sudden scrabbling sound, and two more rabbits burst out of the brush. Lifting the rifle, he killed the first rabbit. The second ran on as he stopped to reload.

"I'll get it," Pa yelled, and broke into a run. Will heard the shot and his father's jubilant shout. He smiled. So there would be three rabbits for supper. Ma wouldn't have to ladle carefully to make sure there was a fair share of the meat in everyone's broth. Tonight, there would be plenty.

"We'll gut and skin these here, son," Pa called.

Will started toward him. All the men had taken to cleaning their game outside camp. It saved the families with less food the torture of watching a long supper preparation. The Hogans were the worst off. Will hated bringing meat into camp, walking past their wagon. They had seven children, and Mr. Hogan was a terrible shot. Back home, he had been a fine farmer, always helping his neighbors in bad years. All the Van Pattens still gave him meat because of that. Otherwise, his children would have starved by now.

For the last month there had been little game to share. Mr. Bailey kept all his meat for himself. Mr. Tolford still gave away some, mostly to the Hogans, but he jerked more meat now and kept it back for himself and Moses, his hired man. They were both good shots. Mr. Tolford's wagons were full of supplies, not bedding and furniture. He had even brought oats for his mule team.

"Gather up some sage, Will." Pa leaned his rifle against a flat rock the size of a bedstead, then pulled his slender skinning knife from its scabbard.

"Yes, sir." Will propped his rifle beside his father's

and laid the rabbits on the rock. Then he headed toward the brush.

The sage stems were hollow and dry and snapped easily. The sharp, clean smell of the leaves tickled at Will's nostrils. When he started back, his father was just finishing the first rabbit. Will spread the sage out so his father could lay the carcass down, pink and glistening, then set the skin to one side. Will broke off a handful of leaves and rubbed them over the still warm meat. It was early, but flies would gather soon.

"Your mother will be glad to see these," Will's father said as he gutted the second rabbit, then made the long, quick cuts that freed the skin.

A faint rustling caught Will's attention. He half-turned, one hand full of sage leaves. Twenty paces away, among the dense papery leaves of a buckwheat bush, he saw a slight movement. Suddenly, a big jackrabbit, twice the size of the cottontails they had killed, rushed into the open.

Whirling, leaning to reach across the rock for his rifle, Will had a split-second daydream of a dramatic, last-second shot, of being the one to bring home enough meat to last into tomorrow. Then he stepped on a rock that rolled beneath his foot. He struggled to keep his balance as he lurched sideways, falling into his father. As he hit the ground he heard his father cry out.

Will scrambled to his feet. His father's face had gone pale, and the knife lay at the base of the rock. There was a slanting gash across his father's thigh.

"What the—? Will, what are you doing?" Pa bent to press his hand over the wound.

Will stood still, shocked by the stream of blood pouring from between his father's fingers. "I was just—I saw a jackrabbit and I was just—"

"Tear some strips from your shirt, Will. Two or three, wide enough to cover this."

Will stared at his father for a second, still stunned by the ivory pallor in his face, the sheen of sweat on his skin.

"Do as I say, Will!"

Will fumbled at his shirttail, his hands shaking. It had all happened so fast. He shrugged his shirt off, then gripped the cloth, hesitating an instant. His entire life it had been drilled into him to take care of the clothing that had cost his mother so many hours to sew. And she sewed well. The hem was sturdy, the stitches so close together that for an eternal moment

Will could not manage to start a tear. Clumsy, frantic, glancing involuntarily at the blood soaking his father's trousers, Will managed to rip a long strip of cloth and extended it toward his father.

"I can't. You'll have to do it, Will." Pa's voice sounded distant, faint. He worked at his suspenders buttons and slid his trousers down. The cut was even deeper than Will had thought. Frightened, Will tore two more bandage strips. He forced himself to concentrate, to push the edges of the gash together, to bind his father's leg tightly. The blood soaked the bandages almost instantly, but once they were tied off, it slowed to a trickle. Pa pulled his trousers up and fastened his suspenders again.

"Finish skinning that last rabbit, son."

Will looked up at the calmness in his father's voice. "I'm sorry, Pa. I'm really sorry. I just thought—"

"We don't have time for that now, Will. Finish the last one, and let's get going."

"Can you walk, Pa?"

His father laughed, an ugly grating sound. "Unless you're going to carry me."

Chapter Two

Jess squatted, careful to keep her skirts away from the little spring. She skimmed the gourd dipper just beneath the surface of the water, trying not to dredge up any of the mossy slime as she refilled the bucket.

"Ma says hurry," Eli called from behind her.

"I can't," Jess answered. "Unless you want to drink mud instead of water."

She glanced up in time to see Eli flash one of his sunny smiles. She grinned back. It was almost impossible to be in low spirits around Eli.

"Jedediah Brancourt, you run on home now," Jess heard Mrs. Hogan call out in her odd accent.

"Jed's probably bothering that old rooster of theirs again," Eli said.

Jess sighed and dropped the gourd into the bucket. "Will you carry this back to camp? I'll go get him."

Eli nodded. "Why does he have to get into so much mischief all the time?"

Jess shrugged. "He's only seven."

Eli smiled. "Was I that much trouble when I was seven?"

Jess hesitated, then shook her head. "But Ma says that Will was a terror when he was little."

Eli picked up the bucket and started walking. It bumped against his knees at every step, but he was careful not to slosh the water.

Jess watched him for a few seconds. He was starting to look skinny and big-footed, like Will before he had shot up tall. But maybe Eli was thin from scant food, not quick growth.

"Will you just leave that old Shanghai rooster alone!" Mrs. Hogan was scolding.

Hoping her mother hadn't heard Mrs. Hogan yet, Jess gathered her skirts and straightened her bonnet, hurrying uphill toward the shout. Making her way through the stand of mesquite at the center of camp, Jess ran along the edge of the big Van Patten camp, waving when Hans smiled at her. Nancy was helping her mother and Jess tried to catch her eye, but couldn't.

The three Van Patten wagons formed a wind shelter for their fire. Jess heard some of the children laughing. She envied them. They hadn't left aunts and uncles and cousins behind—the whole Van Patten family had come west together.

The Hogans were noisy, too. The children were all playing hen and chicks. The baby was asleep on a blanket beneath a bedsheet awning. Dull-eyed oxen stood in the shade of the tattered wagon, their massive heads close together. Just beyond them was an old wire crate. Jed knelt beside it.

Mrs. Hogan stood nearby, her hands on her hips, glaring down at Jed. Her apron was frayed and stained. Her hair poked from beneath her bonnet. The instant she saw Jess, she made a gesture of helplessness.

"I've told him over and over, and he just won't—"

"Shanghai likes me," Jed said, aiming his argument at Jess, not Mrs. Hogan. He had learned there was no point in trying to charm her. She was too busy worrying about her hungry children to be tolerant of a nosy, rooster-loving little boy.

"Mr. Hogan said he was going to kill Shanghai," Jed whined as Jess got close enough to get hold of his sleeve.

Jess glanced up to see Mrs. Hogan nodding. "I've held out as long as I can. Shanghai and both the hens. They haven't laid an egg in weeks, and we haven't got scraps enough to feed them."

"No!" Jed argued sharply.

Mrs. Hogan sighed, shaking her head. "That boy has no manners," she told Jess.

Jess could only shrug, tightening her grip on Jed's sleeve. She leaned close to his ear. "Apologize!"

"I'm sorry, Mrs. Hogan," Jed recited.

She looked at him. "Just leave the chickens alone, Jed. I like old Shanghai, too, but there's nothing to be done about it."

Jess tugged at Jed until he finally lurched sideways, then caught his balance as she got him walking. He shot her a sidelong glance, then wrenched around to look back at the proud little rooster.

"You mind your own business," Jess scolded him.

"But he's going to kill—"

"It's Mr. Hogan's rooster," Jess reminded him. "And those children have got to eat something."

Jed nodded glumly. "Daniel doesn't look right."

"He's been feverish, Jed."

"I wish we could give them more food."

Jess started to answer, then stopped. She wished it, too, but Pa was adamant, and even Ma said he was right. They had to feed themselves first. If Mr. Hogan couldn't provide for his family, he should not have come West.

Jess pulled her brother along, refusing to let him stop and look backward again. "Ma needs more wood," she told him as they passed through the stand of mesquite.

"I brought her armloads this morning," Jeb said. "Eli did, too."

Jess let go of his sleeve. Ma was standing beside the fire, stirring a tub of laundry with the flat paddle Pa had whittled from an oak plank they'd found next to the trail. Jess could see the steam rising. The smell of the lye soap was strong. Her mother's cheeks were flushed with heat, and her eyes were red.

Jess nudged Jed toward the wagon. "Go find Eli and get some more wood. Look out for snakes," she added, knowing that she sounded just like Ma. "Mr. Bailey says we might see some sidewinders soon, and that they're quick and mean." Jed made a face, but he went off in the right direction.

"Jess? Can I get you to lend a hand over here?"

"Sure, Ma," Jess called. She lifted her eyes to scan the eastern horizon. The brush-dotted land was rocky and bleak. There was still no sign of Will or Pa.

"I need you to lift the other end of the lug pole," Ma said.

Jess nodded and gripped it hard, moving steady and slow as the huge pot swung between them. Once they were well clear of the fire, her mother gestured with her chin.

"Right here, Jessamine. I just want it out of the way so the boys don't tumble into it and get scalded." Jess saw her mother glancing eastward and knew what she was thinking before she said it. "I didn't expect them to be gone this long." She smiled. "Maybe they found antelope like the ones back in Mormonie."

"I'd settle for skunk." Jess watched her mother's face, hoping she would laugh. She did, but then worry clouded her eyes again.

"I think most of them are going to take the short-cut with us, Jessamine. But Mr. Bailey says he won't. He wants to head straight south and pick up the

Old Spanish Trail. I'm afraid Mr. Tolford is going to go with him."

Jess scuffed at the ground. "Why can't the men just agree on how we're supposed to go?"

Ma sighed. "They all think they're doing right. If winter hadn't closed the trails that lead west over the mountains, we wouldn't have had all this trouble," she said finally.

Jess knew it was true. But they had gotten delayed, and the snow had fallen on the high passes while they were still at the Salt Lake settlement trying to talk the people into letting them camp there for the winter.

"What I'm tired of," Ma said quietly, "is the endless arguments."

Jess nodded. For the last month, she had fallen asleep most nights listening to two or more of the men wrangle about which route to take.

Mr. Bailey was one of the worst. He and his wife had come from Arkansas. They were rough-spoken, independent people who would rather die than ask for help. They had no children, but Mrs. Bailey had a little dog that she pampered, letting it ride inside the wagon when the weather was bad. Pa couldn't stand the dog. It barked every time it saw him, for some reason.

"Where'd you send Jed?"

Jess turned to face her mother. "I told him to find Eli and gather some more wood."

"I wish we were home and I could send them down to the cellar for some apples and squash."

The dreamy sound in her mother's voice made Jess homesick. Their Illinois farmhouse had someone else living in it now. Pa had sold it—without listening to any of their pleas against it. So someone else was lying in a warm bed tonight, looking out the little window in her loft. Jess fiercely envied whoever it was.

"I could start a pot of beans," Ma said softly. "But I hate to until I see what your father brings."

Jess nodded, not wanting to think about food.

Eli and Jed came trooping back into camp, each one carrying half an armload of grease-wood and mesquite. They were quiet, and Jess could tell they were trying not to laugh.

"Is that all you could find?" Jess asked.

Eli's mouth twitched. Jed frowned thoughtfully. "There's not that much deadwood left close by."

Ma shrugged. "We won't be here but one more night, I hope. Mrs. Bailey is looking more rested today."

"We shouldn't have waited on her," Eli put in, his face suddenly stern. He looked like a miniature of Pa, and Jess almost giggled, waiting for Ma to answer him.

"We most certainly should have," Ma scolded. "Everyone waited while we fixed our wheel on Sublette's cutoff."

Jess grimaced. That cutoff had been the start of all the arguments that had followed. Two weeks later, north of the settlement on Salt Lake, they had split up, some of the men deciding that Oregon land sounded better than California gold. They had met returning miners on the trail—men who had described the hard life in the goldfields and how few struck it rich. Pa had dismissed their warnings. They were either lazy or crazy, he'd said.

"There's Pa and Will!" Eli shouted. He and Jed dropped their wood beside the fire. Eli yelled for a race, and Jed groaned. He never won. Still, as always, he started running, and Eli stayed beside him for a ways before sprinting past.

Jess squinted. As she watched, Pa stopped and bent down, as though he had found something and was picking it up. Will stopped beside him. Jess strained to see what they were doing. Will turned to one side, and she could see for an instant the game bag swinging heavily from his arm.

"They got something," Ma breathed, and Jess nodded.

"Rabbit, maybe."

Ma began to hum, turning back to the fire. She lifted the bucket and poured water into the stew pot. "Those little stinkers didn't bring me enough wood."

Jess turned to smile and nod, then looked back out across the rocky ground. Eli and Jed were getting closer to Pa and Will now. Puzzled, Jess saw them slow, then stop, still a dozen paces away. Why weren't they dancing circles around Will the way they always did? Was something wrong? Maybe Will and Pa hadn't gotten anything at all. Maybe the game bag was empty. Jess frowned. Her stomach knotted.

"Let's get some wood and get the fire built up high," Ma said.

Jess glanced at her and nodded. Pa and the boys were all standing still now.

"Come on, Jess!" Ma scolded, wiping her hands on her apron.

"Ma!" It was Eli. He sounded scared. Jess stood helplessly as Eli ran toward them, his face contorted. "Pa's hurt," he shouted as he got closer. "He's hurt bad."

Chapter Three

As the sun came up, Will lay still, watching his father cross the camp. Ma had washed the blood out of his trousers and mended the tear by firelight. Pa had fibbed to her about how deep the cut was, glancing in Will's direction twice to make sure he kept his mouth shut.

Will rolled over and stared at the pink eastern sky. Except for the worry of Pa being hurt, it had been a good night. The rabbit stew had tasted like heaven. A full belly made for sound sleep, as Ma always said.

"Will? You awake yet?" Pa called, stretching.

Will scrambled out of his bedroll and pulled on his pants. As he buttoned his shirt, he saw Pa stirring last night's coals with a long stick. Will watched him throw on some of the broken deadwood Eli and Jed had collected. It began to smoke, and Pa fanned the fire with his hat.

Will shivered in the chill morning air. "Are we going to leave today, Pa?"

His father shook his head. "Looks like it. Bailey says he's ready to go on this morning."

"But your leg, Pa. Should you—"

"It's nothing, Will. I don't want to hear another word about it. You understand me?"

"Where's Ma?" Will asked quietly.

"She and Jess are down getting water."

Will took a deep breath, sidling up to the welcome warmth of the campfire. "Maybe we should stay a day or two and see if your leg—"

"Get your brothers up, Will. I want them to graze the oxen for an hour or two early—especially if we are going on today. Brownie's hooves are sore, so remind them to take it easy on him."

The tone of his father's voice warned Will to leave off. He glanced at his father's thigh, at the neat row of mending stitches in his trousers. The bloodstain hadn't come out. There was a shadow on the cloth.

"Will? Roust the boys—or are you just planning to stand there until noon?"

Will ducked his head at his father's teasing. "I'm on my way, Pa."

"I want you to start going over the harness, Will. If we end up with another idle day, I want to do any repairs."

Will nodded and started off, then hesitated near the wagon, turning to watch his father walk toward the Baileys' wagon. He was limping.

"Eli!" Will called, slapping the dust-caked Osnaburg cover. "Jed!" Inside the wagon he heard small sounds. Eli usually woke up chipper. Jed was grumpy for the first half hour. "Pa wants you to herd the oxen out to some of the greasewood this morning."

"Are we leaving?" It was Eli. A few seconds later, he emerged, blinking in the early sun. He stepped over the gate and down onto the little platform Pa had built onto the back of the wagon. "Are we?"

Will shrugged. "Pa thinks so."

Eli scuffed at the dirt. His bare feet were stained almost black. "I liked it better when there were more people."

"Me, too," Will admitted.

Jed came over to the wagon gate, his shirt half tucked. He stood silently as he rubbed his eyes, then hitched his pants higher and worked at his trouser buttons. After a few minutes, they went off together, Eli whistling and Jed grousing about being hungry. Will watched them until the big, slow-moving oxen were all headed in the same direction, plodding along in front of the boys. Then he looked up at the sunrise that was flooding the sky with orange and pink.

"Where's your father?" Will heard his mother speak and looked up. She and Jess were coming up the hill from the spring, carrying a bucket of water apiece.

"He went to talk to the other men about what we're going to do today."

"I hope we can get moving," Jess said.

"Me, too," Will agreed. Jess wasn't smiling, but it was hard to tell if she suspected that Pa was hurt worse than he was admitting. Will wished Ma wasn't so close by. He wanted to tell Jess—it was hard to be alone with something as worrisome as this.

"Pa told me it can't be that much farther to California. He thinks this shortcut will save us weeks of travel."

Ma nodded, smiling. "That's what the man who sold him the map said. I can't wait to sleep in a bed."

"It won't be that much longer, Ma," Will said, but had no idea if it was true or not. Pa had talked about ten or fifteen shortcuts now, and he hadn't always been right. He'd been wrong about being able to overwinter at Salt Lake, too. The little Mormon town was so new that the people didn't want to take in strangers.

Ma was scooting the heavy stew pot close to the fire. When she pushed the lug pole through the wire bale, Jess grabbed her end and they lifted together.

"At least we won't start out hungry," Ma said, settling the pot into the bed of coals.

"Eli and Jed are out with the oxen," Will told her as he carried the first span of harness close to the fire. He sat down on a rock and began running the straps between his fingers, snapping the leather hard to test each joining. He looked up every few seconds, watching for his father.

It was Jess who saw Pa first. Will felt her quick nudge and raised his eyes, trying to read his father's face as he approached.

Ma looked up. "The stew is hot, Russell."

"Well, we'd better eat quick, Mary, because we're leaving."

Will heard Jess murmur something, and he turned in time to see her quick smile appear, then vanish. He wanted to be as glad about leaving as she was—but he couldn't. He tried not to glance at the mended tear on his father's trouser leg.

"Are we all going on together?" Ma asked. Will could hear the cautious hope in her question.

"I guess not," Pa said. "The Baileys and the Van Pattens are going south. They refuse to take good advice."

"The Van Pattens?" Will echoed. That meant three wagons and nearly twenty people less. Without them and the Baileys, there would be only four wagons left to take the shortcut together.

"Why are they . . . leaving us?" Ma asked, her hands rubbing anxiously against her apron front.

Pa shrugged. "Like I said, Mary, they just don't want good advice. This shortcut ought to save two or three weeks, which means it'll save lives. The Van Pattens have more small children than any other group. They're fools to take the long way when we've been lucky enough to learn about this new route."

"What if they're right?" Jess blurted, and Will turned to stare at her. She usually said what was on her mind—but not to Pa. No one did. Once he had made up his mind, there was no talking him out of it. He was smiling.

"Jess, honey, just eat your breakfast, then go trade places with Eli and Jed. Will, you finish up the harness, eat, then go with your sister. Your mother and I need to talk."

Will watched him gesture at Ma, then lead her around the other side of the wagon. He listened hard as they went past. "Tolford says he'll stick with us," Pa was saying. "I gave him a copy of the map. . . ."

His hands automatically going about his work, Will tried to hear more, but his father dropped his voice. Jess ladled up two bowls of stew. Will's fingers flew, and he was done checking the harness before his stew stopped steaming. Jess was sitting across from him, her knees bent beneath her full skirts, her hands pressed against her stew bowl.

As Will began to eat, he glanced toward the wagon. He couldn't hear his father talking at all now. That might not be good, he knew. Sometimes when his father was truly angry, he whispered. And if Ma was arguing with him about the shortcut . . .

"You think we're going to make it in the next week or two?" Jess asked.

Will was startled out of his thoughts. He leaned toward her, needing to share his worry with someone. "Pa's leg is cut bad," he whispered to Jess. "Real bad. He's just acting like it doesn't hurt."

Her eyes went wide. "He said it wasn't anything to worry—"

"You two about finished eating?" Pa came toward them, stepping over the wagon tongue.

"It's just now cooled off enough to start, Pa," Jess said quickly. He nodded absently, going right past them and out of camp again. They heard him hail Mr. Tolford.

"Now what?" Jess whispered.

Will could only shake his head, swallowing a mouthful of stew. "I don't know."

They both ate fast. Jess didn't say another word until she asked which direction Eli and Jed had taken the oxen. Will pointed, setting down his empty bowl and glancing toward the wagon.

"Ma's still probably saying good-byes," Jess said.

Will nodded. The good-byes were the hardest part for Ma, he knew. The women always traded keepsakes and wept and promised to write to each other's relatives to try to stay in touch. The men usually stood off to one side after they had shaken hands once.

Eli and Jed had taken the oxen almost a full mile from camp, and it took them a while to get back. By the time Pa sat on the hard bench, the reins in his hand and Ma by his side, Will could tell that Mr. Tolford was irritated at the delay. He kept pulling his high-crowned hat off and picking at a worn place in the felt. He finally shouted, "Ready!" and drove his wagon around them, starting southward. Moses, the hired hand, had hitched up the mule team this morning. The extra oxen plodded along behind.

"Ready now!" Pa shouted. He slapped the reins against the leaders' rumps and touched the wheelers with his whip. Brownie and Becky leaned into their yokes, testing the weight of the wagon, grunting with effort as they got it rolling. Will walked behind the wagon with his brothers and Jess. They had no animals to herd now. All the cattle had been slaughtered or traded before they had even gotten to Salt Lake.

The Baileys and the Van Pattens drew alongside, driving parallel for half a mile before they veered straight southward. At the plodding pace of the oxen, they stayed in sight for three hours, the distance between the two wagon trains widening by inches.

Eli and Jed shouted themselves hoarse, trading farewells with the Van Patten boys who were about their age. Nancy Van Patten stood on the rear step of her wagon, weeping and waving at Jess. The women called back and forth at first, then just waved at each other. Then everyone fell silent and still. Tolford urged his team on, and Moses followed in the second wagon.

Will kept glancing at his father. He seemed determined to keep up with Mr. Tolford. The Hogans brought up the rear as they usually did. Will watched the departing wagons grow smaller, then wink out, like stars when the moon comes up. He heard Jess sigh and knew that she shared the heaviness in his heart. Eli and Jed walked along with their heads down now. Even the Hogan children were quiet. The endless rocky country around them was so empty. The wagons seemed as small as whittled toys.

Chapter Four

The next day, Jess began to think Pa had made the right decision. Everything seemed to be going well. They found a spring at noon and another, fifteen miles farther on, where they camped for the night. Mr. Tolford and Moses rode two of the mules into the hills to the west and shot and killed two wild sheep. There was enough meat to feed everyone supper, then breakfast in the morning.

After breakfast, Jess helped her mother repack their kitchen, then walked behind the wagon with Will again. They were heading southwest now, and Mr. Tolford led the wagons at a brisk pace. His oxen were stronger than anyone else's because he had three teams and one was always at rest.

At noon, they stopped without finding water.

Mr. Hogan drove his team into the scant shade of some mesquite trees. Jess followed her family's wagon a hundred yards farther. Pa climbed down off the driver's bench, then helped Ma to the ground.

"I'm hungry," Jed complained.

"Hush and help your mother," Pa answered sharply. Then he looked at Jess. "You, too. I'm going to go talk to Tolford. The pace he's setting is going to kill our animals."

Jess watched him walk away. He had been snappish all day long. She glanced at Will and caught him staring at Pa, too, his eyes narrowed.

"What?"

Will shook his head. "Nothing, I guess. I think he's trying not to limp." The last sentence was a whisper.

"Maybe it hurts, but that doesn't mean it won't heal quickly," Jess murmured low enough so Eli and Jed couldn't hear her. Ma was still fussing with her bonnet strings, stretching and marching in place to ease her cramped legs.

At the edge of the brush, Pa turned and cupped his hands around his mouth. "Will? Why don't you come with me?"

Will took off, half-running, to catch up with Pa. Jess watched them both, trying to discern a limp in her father's stride. He seemed to be keeping his right leg straighter than usual, she thought. Nothing more.

"Do you have any water you could spare?"

Jess turned to see Mrs. Hogan standing with a bucket in her hand. Her eyes were intense, and she spoke rapidly, barely pausing for breath.

"We thought that the springs would be close enough together that we could get away without filling all the water barrels last night. That's what your father said—that the shortcut had water every fifteen miles."

Jess pulled in a deep breath. "You'll have to ask Pa."

Mrs. Hogan frowned. "Of course, of course." She set down the bucket, then picked it up again. "My husband wouldn't fill the barrels. He said there was no reason to wear out the oxen hauling water when the springs would be so close together."

Jess looked at her helplessly. She knew Pa would be angry if they gave away water without asking. She also knew that if Mrs. Hogan asked him, there was little chance he'd give her any.

"Is there something the matter, Vera?" Ma called.

Mrs. Hogan shook her head, then she nodded. "Mr. Hogan only filled the barrels halfway and he's given most of it to the oxen. I know I won't have enough to give the children a drink now, and still cook this evening."

Jess saw her mother glance off in the direction Pa and Will had gone. Then she turned to pry the lid from the water barrel. Using their ladle, she gave Mrs. Hogan about a third of a bucket full. Mrs. Hogan took it and walked away quickly.

"Don't say anything about this to your father, please, Jess," Ma said softly.

"I wouldn't," Jess assured her.

"I'm thirsty," Eli said.

"I'm still hungry, Ma," Jed added.

"I've got beans soaking for supper," Ma said. "And just enough biscuits to go around. So you'll have to settle for dried apples."

Eli wrinkled up his nose. "I'm sick of those old apples."

"You ought to be grateful we have anything at all," Ma said wearily, "and that we are all still well and safe."

She had said it at least a hundred times already,

and Jess knew she was right. They had passed so many graves. "Apples sound good to me, Ma," she said, ignoring Eli's frown.

"Me, too," Jed said, and Jess tousled his hair.

"I want bread," Eli muttered.

"We all do, Eli," Ma said. "But we just don't have any."

"I'll get the bag of apples," Jess put in before Eli could say anything else. She was as tired of apples as he was, but it wasn't going to do any good to complain. She glanced westward as she rounded the back of the wagon. There were odd, jagged hills ahead, scattered with trees. Maybe California wasn't much farther. Maybe just another week or so of sleeping on the cold, hard ground.

Will stood beside his father. Mr. Tolford was shaking his head.

"I see no reason why I should slow down and risk my own life because you people insist on carrying a household across the continent. I've told you before, I think you're crazy to be bringing women and children into this—"

"That may very well be your opinion," Pa interrupted. "But the fact remains—"

"The facts are simple," Mr. Tolford said. "You can't keep up. And Hogan is worse yet. Where there was a lot of game and plenty of water, it didn't matter much. But we are in dry country now. Look at it." He made a sweeping gesture with one hand. "If a man is thirsty long enough he gets muddled, stupid. I've heard stories of men dying thirty feet from water because they couldn't think straight and didn't see it."

Will lifted his eyes to the bleak hills that loomed ahead. They did look forbidding. The rock was sharp and barren, patched with snow. But there were ways through them. That's what the man had told Pa. It'd be much easier than going straight west through the massive snow-covered mountains—and shorter than the long Spanish Trail the rest of the wagons had taken.

"You said you'd stick with us when I copied the map for you." Pa's face was grim.

Tolford was shaking his head again. "No, sir, I did not. I said I'd come with you, not stick with you. Not if it means slowing down to a crawl. I mean to get to the goldfields by spring. I want to be working a claim before the—"

"We all want that," Pa broke in.

Will glanced back and forth between the men. Pa's fists were balled up in anger. Tolford's shoulders were squared. For a few seconds, Will thought they might start fighting. Then, his father spat on the ground and turned aside.

"You are welcome to follow along," Tolford said in a reasonable tone. "I certainly wish you well. Hogan, too."

"Thank you, sir," Pa said stiffly. "We surely do appreciate that."

Will watched Tolford stride away, resettling his high-crowned hat. Moses fell in behind him as he passed them.

"What are we going to do, Pa?" Will asked.

"Do?"

Will tried to hold up under his father's scrutiny, but he finally had to look away. "I just meant I wondered what you had planned, Pa."

Will followed when his father started walking. He was silent for so long, Will was sure he was going to ignore the question, but then he spoke.

"We'll stick to the shortcut. No turning around now or later. That's how folks get into trouble, Will. They're afraid to make a decision and stand by it."

"Yes, sir," Will said.

"You're a good boy, Will," Pa told him.

Will saw Mr. Hogan coming and he made a little gesture to alert Pa.

"You tell Tolford to slow up?" Mr. Hogan asked as he got closer.

Will watched his father kick at a stone, then look up at the sky. "I am not in much of a position to tell Tolford anything. I *asked* him, and he said no."

Mr. Hogan took off his hat and rubbed one hand across his forehead. "He just flat refused?"

When Pa didn't respond, Mr. Hogan caught Will's eye. "He wants to get to the goldfields by spring," Will said, not knowing what else to say.

"My oxen are about to give out, and I don't have but two extra animals still fit to work."

"I'm in worse shape, Hogan," Pa said evenly. "We have no extra oxen at all. The point is we have exactly two choices. Keep up with Tolford as best we can and hope he won't abandon us if we hit real trouble, or turn back and try to catch up with Bailey and Van Patten." He paused a few seconds, then spat again. "I'm not turning back. If the man was right about this shortcut, it won't be long till we're into good game country again."

Will studied Mr. Hogan's face as Pa spoke. It was impossible to tell what he was thinking, but Will could guess. Even country with plentiful game didn't guarantee food for his family. What he needed was generous friends who could shoot straighter than he could. Without answering, Mr. Hogan turned on his heel and walked away.

"He's not our worry," Pa muttered, facing the mountains west of them and refusing to meet Will's eyes. "We have to take care of ourselves now."

Will nodded, swallowing hard. Pa was right, but somehow it felt wrong to have to hear it out loud like this. Will stared at the side of his father's face. There was a ridge over his jaw that made Will think he was angry at first, or maybe ashamed of what he had said to Mr. Hogan.

Then Will noticed Pa rubbing at his thigh, pushing gingerly at the wound beneath the mended tear—and he understood. Pa was in pain.

Chapter Five

For the rest of the day, Will had kept an eye on the Hogan wagon. They dropped behind, but never completely out of sight. Still, by the time they caught up and camped it was pitch-dark and the youngest children were already asleep. Mrs. Hogan didn't even bother to build a campfire. Will wondered if they had any food left at all.

This morning, everyone had risen before dawn, and the Hogans, because they hadn't unpacked anything, were the first to pull out of camp for once. Pa had left right behind them. Will and Jess had walked, the boys had ridden inside the wagon—Eli because he had a stomachache, and Jed to keep him company playing checkers.

Mr. Tolford's wagons soon caught up and passed

them all, and Will noticed leather boots tied on the oxen's hooves. Within an hour, the Hogans had fallen behind again, even though Mr. Hogan was whipping his team almost constantly, making a real effort to keep up the pace. Will longed to stride along behind Tolford's wagons, to cover the ground faster. Brownie and Becky and the rest of their oxen were sore-footed and slow.

There was no shade where they stopped midday. After a quick dinner of cold beans and dried apples, everyone just sat quietly in the sun for a half hour. They had little water—none at all to give the oxen. Pa got out his wallet and unfolded the map the man in Salt Lake had drawn for him.

"So that's supposed to be a spring?" Mr. Hogan asked, tapping the wrinkled paper.

Pa nodded. "We should be close. I thought we would have gotten there by now. We're supposed to hit the spring a couple miles before we head north-west into a canyon." He studied the paper.

"We can only hope the map is accurate," Mr. Hogan said quietly.

Mr. Tolford shot him an impatient look. "Several men confirmed the shortcut, Hogan."

"I certainly saw no reason to distrust the man—" Pa began.

"He sold you the map, though, didn't he?" Mr. Hogan asked.

Pa nodded slowly. "That doesn't mean it isn't accurate, does it? All the landmarks he put in have been where they were supposed to be."

Mr. Hogan straightened up, shading his eyes. "I don't like the looks of this country."

No one else said anything, and Will felt Pa nudge his arm. "I guess we'll get going, then. Will, go tell your ma we'd best get packed up."

Mr. Tolford nodded and turned away. Mr. Hogan fell into step beside Pa.

"Makes me uneasy that your map showed a spring that isn't here."

Pa stopped so short that Will almost bumped into him. "We could be half a mile from it," he said angrily.

Mr. Hogan shrugged. "I am not insulting you, Brancourt, just questioning the map, that's all. I can't afford a mistake."

"None of us can," Pa shot back at him, and turned toward the wagon. Will followed at his heels. Their water was almost gone, he was sure. Ma had told

Jed and Eli to suck on pieces of wood to keep their mouths from getting so dry. Will was thirsty, too, but he didn't want to ask for a drink. It scared him to think about the barrels being empty.

Mr. Tolford got his team moving first. He wasn't whipping them on today like he had for the past two days, Will noticed. Maybe he was out of water, too. The hills around them were getting steeper, rockier. Eli and Jed still rode in the wagon, but Jess walked like she always did, and Will was glad to have her company. She didn't complain or even mention being thirsty, and he was grateful for that, too.

As the afternoon passed, the oxen plodded along, their heavy heads low, swinging slightly with each step. Will walked in rhythm with them, not speaking to Jess, just lost in the endless cadence of the oxen's hooves.

"There it is!" Pa shouted.

Will raised his head.

"There! See those trees? There has to be water up there."

Will ran his tongue over his lips. Water. The word made his heart lift.

"I'm thirsty," Will heard Eli saying. There were

other people talking now, too. It was as if everyone was coming out of a trance, awakened by that single word—"water." Will saw Jess veer toward the little stand of trees Pa had pointed at. Tolford was pulling his team to that side.

"Run on up there, Will," Pa called back along the side of the wagon. "See that Tolford doesn't let his animals muddy it."

Will started uphill, following Jess. Mr. Tolford was whipping his oxen into a shuffling jog and yelling something Will couldn't understand to Moses. Rills of dust rose from the oxen's heavy hooves. Will heard Pa shouting at him, and he tried to run faster, but it was hard. The sand was deep and loose, and he was tired. They had been walking since sunup. He caught up with Jess and passed her.

Jess tried to keep up with Will as he went by, but it was impossible. Will's legs were longer, and he didn't have a skirt to fight with as he slogged through the sand. Her bonnet slipped to one side and she pulled it off, lifting her skirts higher.

"Wait up, Mr. Tolford," Will was shouting. "Pa says to be careful not to muddy it before we get our barrels filled up. Everyone needs water and . . ." Will trailed off.

Jess ran on, realizing why Will had stopped yelling. Mr. Tolford was already pulling his oxen to a stop, fighting to keep them under control. They could smell the water, Jess was sure. They sidled in their harness as he leaped from the driver's bench and walked alongside the team, slapping at their faces until they stood still, obeying him. He waited until Moses had brought the other wagon close and had jumped down to hold the reins of both teams. Then he walked toward the spring.

Will was almost to the base of the clumped bushes and trees. Breathing hard, Jess sprinted, ignoring the bruising pain of the rock through the thin soles of her shoes. She managed to pound up behind Will just as Mr. Tolford approached from the other side.

"It's not too deep," Mr. Tolford announced.

Breathing hard, Jess stepped to one side to see past Will. The spring was small, but the water looked clear and cool. Mr. Tolford was kneeling beside it, cupping his hands. Will had dropped to his knees, too, and was leaning forward when Mr. Tolford spewed out the mouthful of water he had taken and coughed. "Damnation!" he lamented. "It's alkali!"

Will looked up, then back down at the water. Jess squatted and wet her fingers, touching them to her lips. The water was cool. It was bitter, but not as bad as some of the water they'd run into in the country around Fort Laramie. She scooped up a little more, her whole body aching for a long drink.

"Don't swallow much," Will warned her. "You'll get sick."

"We may as well see if the animals can drink it," Mr. Tolford said. "Another day without water will kill them, anyway."

Jess saw her father walking toward them and noticed how much he was favoring his right leg. She saw his face fall as Mr. Tolford told him about the sour spring. She glanced back down the bottom of the rocky valley. The Hogans were just now coming into sight.

Jess fought an urge to cry. Will and her father were grim-faced, both of them glancing at the wagon where Ma and the boys were waiting for water. Pa finally started toward them.

"I'll let one of my animals drink all it wants," Mr. Tolford was saying, slapping the dust out of his hat.

"We'll wait and see what happens to it. If the animals can drink, so can we, if we don't drink much."

The words spun in Jess's mind. They had finally found water and they couldn't drink. She heard Jed's high wailing sound and knew that her father had told Ma and the boys about the spring.

Chapter Six

Jess stared at her father and Mr. Hogan. They were standing toe-to-toe, glaring at each other. The rest of the Hogan clan waited by their wagon, a little ways off. Ma and the boys were just beyond them, repacking some blankets that Ma had set out to air. Will had come to stand beside Jess, far enough away so no one would notice them—but close enough to hear what was going on.

"You are out of your mind," Pa was saying very slowly.

Mr. Hogan shook his head. "You're risking your children's lives in order to save a little time and you have the gall to call me crazy?"

"Are you ready?"

Jess turned to look at Mr. Tolford, shouting with

his hands cupped around his mouth. His oxen had all drunk the sour water now, and he was ready to get moving. Pa had let their oxen drink, too, after Mr. Tolford's experiment had proved the water wasn't bad enough to hurt the big animals. Pa had filled the water barrels as well, but he hadn't let Jess or the boys drink more than a mouthful or two to start with, just to be safe.

"I said, are you ready down there?" Mr. Tolford shouted.

Jess looked at Pa again. His face was flushed, and his eyes were hard and angry.

"I'm sorry for any problem it causes—" Mr. Hogan began, but Pa cut him off.

"You can't hope to catch up to the Baileys and the Van Pattens now, you know that."

Mr. Hogan nodded. "But I can follow their tracks and I have more faith in the old Spanish trail than this new one of yours."

"The man said the Chaguanosos have brought horses through here for years. You've heard of them, haven't you? They sell stock all over the Mississippi Valley."

Jess watched Mr. Hogan shrug. "Maybe they know

the way. Or maybe that fellow who sold you the map made up the whole story."

"Hogan," Pa said quietly. "You can't shoot and you can't trap. How are you going to feed your family?"

"I'm more afraid of thirst than hunger, Brancourt," Mr. Hogan said. "And there's not going to be game where you're headed, anyway. Look at this country." He spread his arms to take in the arid hills, the sandy floor of the narrow valley they were in.

Jess watched her father follow the gesture, frowning. "But if you start back now, you'll never—"

"I have two days' supply of the sour water. That'll get me close to that camp where the spring was good. I'll feed the oxen greasewood branches for a day or two, then kill one if I have to, to feed the children. Then I can—"

"You're a fool," Pa cut in. Jess wished he would listen to Mr. Hogan. No one knew what was up ahead. At least the Hogans would be going back to a trail that other people had traveled.

"Look at that," Mr. Hogan said abruptly, pointing.

Jess turned to see Mr. Tolford's two wagons starting off single file.

"I can't keep up with him, and neither can you.

He'll leave if things get bad enough, even if you manage to stay close."

Jess saw her father's face cloud with anger and worry. "Well, I intend to try, Hogan," he said bluntly. "Going back is more foolhardy than going onward at this point. And if the map is true, we'll get to California two weeks or more before you do."

"If you get there at all," Mr. Hogan said, turning on his heel and walking toward his wagon. He shouted at his children to load up.

"Get your brothers into the wagon," Pa said to Jess as he passed. She glanced up the valley. Tolford's wagons were rumbling along at a fast clip again. Tolford was smart. Every time the wagons stopped to rest, he would have Moses cut brush and greasewood for the oxen to eat as they stood in the harness. They had stayed in better flesh than anyone else's.

"Come on, Jess," Will mumbled. "We have to get going."

She nodded, and they started for the wagon. She glanced back once to see her father limping behind them. He looked remote, preoccupied, like a man alone with his thoughts.

"I'm scared," Jess whispered, and Will reached out to grip her shoulder for a moment.

"We'll be all right, I think. But I hope we don't get too far behind Tolford."

"I'm going to cut greasewood for the oxen every chance I get," Jess said.

Will nodded. "It can't hurt."

"Haw!" Jess heard Mr. Hogan shouting as he pulled his team around in a tight curve to the left.

"Move along, you two," Pa said as he passed them, his strides long and uneven.

"What's Mr. Hogan doing?" Ma called out as they got close.

"Turning back," Pa answered curtly.

Ma's eyes widened, but she held her tongue, shooing the boys up over the wagon gate and going to climb onto the bench. Jess and Will took their places behind the wagon. It still felt strange to Jess—not having any extra oxen or cattle to herd—and it was boring. Sometimes it was hard to walk as slowly as the oxen.

Pa cracked the whip over the team, shaking the reins savagely. The oxen started off slowly as they always did, ignoring his bluster. Halfway up the valley, Jess looked back. The Hogans' team was plodding along in the opposite direction, their wagon swaying over the uneven sand. Only then did Jess realize she hadn't said good-bye to any of them.

Will stretched. It was awful to wake up and realize that they were alone. Pa finally had decided to camp, even though they hadn't managed to even catch sight of Tolford before dusk. By the time they had stopped, there was little light left.

True to her resolve, Jess had scrambled up the rocky slope with the hand ax and had come back dragging greasewood and buckwheat brush. The oxen had nibbled at it, their heads low with weariness. Ma had fed everyone the last of the beans and a few dried apples each.

"You awake?" Will asked quietly.

"Yes," Jess said without opening her eyes. "I've just been thinking."

Will rubbed his face. "About what?"

Jess shook her head. "I'm worried about the Hogans."

Will sat up. "I know. But there isn't much we can do, is there?"

"I'm worried about us, too," Jess whispered.

Will pretended not to hear her and stretched again. "Maybe we'll catch up to Tolford today. Maybe he'll bog down, or break a spoke or something."

Jess turned onto her side. "I don't like being all by ourselves like this. What if Indians decide to—"

"We haven't seen Indians in three months," Will said quickly, cutting her off. "And the last time we did, they gave us meat." He didn't want to find one more thing to worry about.

"Let's get started, you two," Pa said, wincing as he stepped down out of the wagon. Will heard stirring inside, and Jed's sleepy voice, then Ma's, answering him.

Will pulled on his clothes, swallowing painfully. His throat was so dry, it hurt. "Can we drink some of the water now, Pa?" he asked.

"Please?" Jess put in. "I didn't even get an upset stomach from it. I think it's good to drink; it just tastes bad."

Pa was facing away from them, staring up the valley, and when he turned, Will saw a patch of dark reddish stain on his trousers. The wound was seeping through the heavy twilled cloth.

"You all right, Pa?" Will asked.

Pa nodded, shifting his weight onto his hurt leg, then quickly back off it again. "It's sore, that's all. It'll heal quick enough." His tone was even and firm like always, but Will noticed yesterday's flush had left Pa's face. Now, he looked pale.

It took an hour for them to get moving. Will tried to hurry, but it was hard. His belly was cramped with hunger, and Ma's ration of dried apples only seemed to make it worse. Jed was whining almost constantly now, and it rubbed everyone raw, even Ma.

"Ready?" Pa called.

"Ready!" Jess yelled back at him, like one driver would answer another. Will felt like hugging her. She had dragged buckwheat branches down to the oxen as soon as she had gotten her clothes on. He looked at her sidelong. Her head was up, her mouth was set in a straight line. He knew all of her expressions and he knew exactly what this one meant. She was as scared as he was.

Chapter Seven

The next day was hotter. The hills seemed to trap the glare of the sun, heating up the narrow valley they were in. Around three o'clock, Jess caught a glimpse of Tolford's wagons, tiny moving dots at the limit of her vision. Still, the sight cheered her. She walked along, spirits a little brighter than they had been since Tolford had left them behind. The rock on the hillsides angled sharply now, striped with ridges of different-colored minerals. The sand beneath her feet was soft and deeper than it had been. It made hard going, and the oxen had slowed.

"Whoa up! Haw, haw there!" Pa shouted. Jess heard the whip crack. She saw Will sprint out to one side, and she knew he was trying to see what was going on. She followed him, racing to keep up when he veered toward the front of the wagon.

"Haw, dang it! Pull, you lazy beasts! Pull!" Pa bellowed.

Jess glanced at the wagon as she ran. The wheels were barely turning in the foot-deep sand. Then she saw the wheeler oxen and nearly cried out. They were almost up to their bellies in sand. The leaders were in deeper yet.

Pa kept shouting, kept cracking the whip, but now that the oxen had stopped there was no way for them to get the wagon moving again. Pa stood up on the footrest and ripped his hat off, throwing it down hard, cursing under his breath. He turned, a jerky, angry movement. As he stepped down, he lost his footing in the sand and lurched to one side, sprawling on the ground. He stood up in a fury, spitting sand out of his mouth.

Jess glanced at Will. He was staring at Pa. Ma was standing on the footrest now, the reins in her hands, shouting to Pa. The oxen were looking around, some of them bawling. Eli's and Jed's high, excited squeals came from inside the wagon.

"Be still!" Pa shouted. "All of you, just be still now!"

Everyone fell silent. Only the bawling of the oxen went on, a forlorn and awful sound. Pa was walking along the length of the hitch, sinking into the loose sand, dragging at the lead pair, trying to get them to move. For a full minute, Jess watched her father struggle in the deep sand. Then he collapsed.

Will started forward, and Jess followed him as Ma screamed and clambered off the bench. She ran the first few steps, then had to slow to marching pace, lifting her feet clear of the sand. Pa struggled to his feet, yelling at her to stay back. He staggered toward her and they stood, knee-deep in the loose sand, holding each other.

Will came to a stop at the edge of the sand bog, and Jess stood beside him. "Is Pa—?" Jess began.

"His leg is bad," Will said sharply.

"Will!" Ma called. "Give us a hand here."

Jess stood trembling as Will made his way toward Ma. He positioned himself beneath Pa's right arm. With Ma on the other side, they walked Pa out of the sand. He took two heavy steps on his own, then sank down again. Jess knew she should do something to help, but her whole body was shaking now.

"See to your brothers, Jess," Ma snapped. Then

she faced Will. "We need to get your father settled. Then we'll worry about the wagon." She turned a slow circle, pulling her bonnet forward to shade her eyes. "Up there," she said, pointing. "See the flat place? It's sandy, not rocky. If we have to camp a day or two—"

"We aren't staying here, Mary," Pa interrupted. They all turned to look at him. He heaved himself into a sitting position. His face was so flushed, Jess wondered if he was feverish.

"You aren't fit to travel, Russell," Ma pleaded.

He stood up, swaying. Will stepped forward, but Pa waved him back. "I'll walk up there and rest awhile. Then we'll figure out what to do about the wagon." He grimaced as he took a step, and Jess wondered how much pain he was in. Pa never complained; he never got sick.

Ma whirled to face Jess. "I told you to see to the boys. Get a blanket out of the wagon and tell your brothers they can get out if they stay close."

Jess started for the wagon, feeling almost dizzy with fear. How could they stay here? But how could they go on if Pa was sick?

"What's wrong with Pa?" Eli demanded, leaning

over the wagon gate, trying to see. Jed echoed him, trying to push his way forward.

"He doesn't feel well," Jess said carefully. There was no point in scaring them. "Ma says you can get out, but leave Pa alone and stay close. No one has time to keep track of you now."

"We can help," Eli said, and he sounded so brave and steady that Jess wanted to hug him.

"Bring me a blanket, then," she told him. He disappeared into the wagon, then emerged a few seconds later, carrying Pa's favorite—one that had belonged to Grandma Tate.

"Thanks, Eli," Jess said, managing to smile at him. "Be careful of the deep sand and stay right by the wagon. I'll come get you if Ma needs more help."

Jess was surprised to see how far Will and Ma had gotten with Pa. They were almost to the flat place. By the time she got there with the blanket, Pa was sitting down, bent forward, his eyes closed.

A few feet away, Ma was clearing rocks and pebbles, sweeping them aside with her hands. "Lay it out over here."

Jess folded the blanket lengthwise. She and Will held the corners down while Pa sat sideways, then twisted around to lie back, wincing and breathing heavily. Ma watched anxiously as he shifted, trying to get comfortable. She pressed her hand against his forehead. "Russell, you have a fever." She straightened, and Jess saw her glancing at Pa's leg. "I think I should take a look at that wound."

"No, it's fine, don't worry about it." Pa tried to sit up, but she gripped his shoulders and eased him back onto the blanket. "Russell, it isn't fine. Your limp is worse every day."

"But, Mary—"

"I won't hear another word about it. I am going to clean the wound and get a fresh bandage on it." Ma was rolling up Pa's trouser leg, and Jess found that she couldn't look aside. Her father caught his breath as Ma pulled the dirty bandage off. Jess stared. The wound was angry red and swollen. A trickle of yellowish fluid seeped from it.

"Jess?" At Will's voice, she looked up into his eyes. "Ma can do this," he said quietly. "Let's go get the wagon out if we can."

Jess nodded, glancing once more at Pa's wound. The cut itself was a blackish line.

Ma spoke without turning. "Do that. And send Eli

up here with my extra petticoat and a bucket of water."

Will nudged Jess into starting downhill. She heard the thin, high howling of coyotes in the distance.

For quite a while, Will was able to avoid thinking about how they were actually going to get the wagon out. First, he'd had the boys help unload everything. Then he and Jess had set about unhitching the team.

The lead pair and second pair had been the hardest. The oxen were balky and scared of the sand that brushed their bellies. The third and fourth pairs were easier. Jess had just gotten on one of each hitch, flailing at their flanks with a stick while Will heaved on their lead ropes to make them flounder sideways, turning back to wade out of the deep sand. Will led the fifth pair back without Jess's help.

As the oxen were unhitched, Eli and Jed herded them into a stand of buckwheat brush. Once they stopped shaking and bawling, they began to graze.

"Now what?" Jess asked.

Will looked at her. "I don't know," he confessed. "I guess we can see if the wheelers can pull it out now that it's empty. Maybe they can."

Jess was squinting at the sun. "We have two hours of daylight, if that."

Will shrugged, glancing up the hill one more time. Ma was still sitting by Pa, facing away from the wagon. What were they talking about?

"Maybe we should go ask Pa what to do next," Jess said quietly.

Will shook his head. "They're depending on me. On both of us. Pa needs to rest. I just wish we had something to make for supper."

Jess nodded. "Ma has that little bit of flour left. I could make hoecakes."

Will looked downhill at the little herd of oxen. Eli and Jed were standing quietly, letting the tired animals graze. "Let's see what the wheelers can do. You drive."

Will watched as Jess climbed up onto the bench. She loved to drive the team, and Pa almost never let her. "They're so tired," Jess said as he positioned himself by Becky's head. He nodded, his eyes flickering back and forth.

The wooden wagon wheels were in loose sand about six inches deep. The oxen were standing only eight or so feet farther into the sand bog—but it came up nearly to their hocks.

Will stood, puzzling it out. The oxen would have to angle to the side. But how sharp a turn could they make without ruining the whiffle-tree or pulling the wagon over on its side? "Wait," he said to Jess. She lowered the reins.

Becky was stronger than Brownie. If they could get her moving, she might pull him along. Will took Becky's muzzle in his right hand and leaned against the side of her face, shoving her head around as far as she would let him. "Now!" he called to Jess.

Jess began to shout and cajole the two exhausted oxen, shaking the reins and cracking the whip off to the right side. Will kept pushing. Jess cracked the whip again, closer this time, and he realized what she was doing. Instead of snapping it over the oxen's backs, she was popping it as loudly as she could near their ears, hoping they'd shy away from it—and into a sharper turn.

As Will shoved and Jess shouted, Becky began to move, first leaning forward in the harness, testing the weight of the wagon behind her. She was not used to pulling anything without five pairs of oxen hitched in front of her, and Will could feel her reluctance. He set his shoulder against hers and heaved, shouting. He stumbled when Becky took her first wholehearted step to the side, forcing Brownie to move with her.

"Haw!" Jess screamed, cracking the whip and shaking the reins frantically. Becky took another step, and Will shoved her hard. He glanced back. The wagon tongue was angled now, but not quite far enough. If the arc of the turn carried the wagon too far forward—and into the deeper sand—he was afraid it would tip. Becky bawled, the yoke jabbing at her shoulder as she leaned into the harness.

"Haw," Jess was pleading, standing on the footrest now and keeping up a steady stream of shouted encouragement.

Becky took another ponderous step, and Will heard the front wheels turn, grinding against the ground. He saw the edge of a rock as the sand shifted. Just then the left wheel rose, tilting the wagon. He yelled at his sister, "Sit down!"

Jess fell backward as the wagon lurched, but she never let up in her stream of hollering, and the whip cracked every few seconds, popping like gunfire as she scrambled back to her feet. The oxen were really pulling now.

Will let Becky take the next step at less of an angle,

then he got out of her way altogether and stood back to watch his sister drive the wagon in a short semi-circle, not stopping until it was well clear of the sand that had almost trapped them. It was only then that he heard Eli and Jed cheering and looked up the hill. Ma was waving one hand above her head.

Chapter Eight

Jess thought they'd never get around the sand bog, but they finally had managed it. The day after that, Will had killed the weakest ox. It had been so skinny that the meat had lasted only two days. Will had jerked the last thirty pounds, smoking long, thin strips over the fire until it was dry. Ma parceled it up and squirreled it away in the wagon.

As the days went on, Jess became more worried. Pa was no better. If anything, he was worse. Ma had set up a sunshade—a three-sided tent made of bedsheets and blankets. Will had taken the rifle and walked the valley for several miles, ranging up the sides of the mountains to look for game. He had only seen birds, and those had been too high or too quick to risk a shot. But he had found something more important than food: a spring.

It had taken them two days to reach it. They had filled the water barrels to the top and rested a day, killing the next weakest ox. Then they had gone on again, still following Tolford's wagon tracks. As they traveled, the soft sandy ground gave way to rougher, rocky country. In three days, their water was almost gone again, but they kept going.

On Christmas Day, Jess sat on the driver's bench next to Will. Ma was in the wagon with Eli and Jed—and Pa, who lay feverish and flushed on a stack of blankets.

Jess's mouth was dry all the time now—the valley had narrowed, and it felt more like July than December. The oxen walked slowly, their sides heaving. Some of them lolled their tongues out. Jess hated looking at them. As the wagon jolted along she could hear Pa moaning, and Ma's soothing voice.

The trail got rockier. They had been able to see Tolford's wheel tracks all morning, but now the uneven ground was graveled and littered with bigger stones and boulders. As the wagon wheels rolled over the melon-sized rocks, dropping back down,

Will kept the whip popping almost constantly.

Jess looked at her brother. His face had changed. His cheeks had hollowed out, and his lips had bloody cracks in them. His hands were scratched and gouged by the rough bark of the greasewood they had been cutting for the oxen every chance they got. Jess studied her own hands. They looked just like Will's.

The wagon lurched upward, then banged down, and Jess had to grip the edge of the seat with both hands. "How much farther to the next spring?" she asked Will and was astonished when he smiled.

He pointed. "The map made it look like a long ways yet. But see those mesquite trees?"

Jess shaded her eyes. There was a long oval of green brush running down a slope. She nodded, feeling hope blossom inside her heart. The idea of having enough water to drink her fill made her almost dizzy with happiness.

"Don't say anything yet," Will cautioned. "Just in case."

Jess nodded. He was right. There was no point in getting Ma and the boys excited until they were sure. She held her breath, staring at the greenery as it slowly got closer. Then she saw the lead oxen throw their massive heads back, their eyes rimmed with white.

"They smell water," Will said quietly.

Jess watched him take the slack out of the reins and brace his feet on the footrest. But as the team got closer to the spring, it was no use. They shuffled into a clumsy trot, hauling the wagon, lurching and banging, over jagged rock. Jess stared at the ground as the driver's bench jolted and pitched, wondering if she could jump clear and sprint to the front to startle the oxen into slowing down. But the wicked-looking rocks covered the sand. Even if she managed to land without hurting herself, she would never be able to run fast enough. The wagon heaved back and forth, the rims of the wheels gritting over the rocks.

"Will? What are you doing?" Ma called from inside the wagon.

"I think there's water up here, Ma," Will said over his shoulder. "The team can smell it."

Just as he said it, Jess felt the front of the wagon lifting upward. Then it smashed downward, and the rear wheels lifted. Jess braced herself, praying that Pa's blanket bed was thick enough to keep him from being bruised by the slamming of the wagon. She could tell that Will had given up trying to guide the team and was just hoping to hold them in. There was little else he could do now. They had stopped responding to his calls of gee and haw, or even the snapping of the whip.

Without warning, the right side of the wagon tilted upward, and Jess clutched at the bench to keep from sliding. She heard her mother shout something to Eli and Jed, then the wagon crashed down again and slewed sideways. There was a sharp squeal, then a splintering sound.

Will stood and shouted at the oxen. He leaped from the bench, tossing the reins toward Jess. She wrapped them around the brake handle as the oxen stumbled to a stop, confused by the sudden heaviness of the wagon. Then she sat still, trembling, fearing the worst. A few seconds later, Will was back, his face somber. "It's the axle," he whispered to her. "Broke clean in half, almost." He slammed his fist into the bench, and Jess saw blood on his knuckles.

Jess couldn't speak. She couldn't think of anything to say. She looked past Will, at the endless misshapen hills. They were in the middle of badlands, Pa was sick, they had nowhere to get food except for killing more of the oxen and . . .

"Was it the axle?" Ma said quietly, poking her head out of the wagon cover. Will lowered his eyes, and Jess had to tell her.

"Yes, Ma." Jess watched her mother's lips begin to move and knew she was praying.

Late that night, Will stared into the campfire. Pa was so feverish, it was hard to tell if he had even understood what had happened. They had carried him out of the wagon again, after they'd set up camp by the spring. Now he was settled on his bed of blankets, with Ma lying beside him beneath their quilt. Jess was sleeping, too. Eli and Jed finally had stopped whispering, and Eli was snoring, a soft little-boy snore.

Will stood up and walked numbly to the edge of the camp. There was a fat crescent moon hanging low in the east. Tolford's wagon tracks were clearly visible in its silvery light. But it was hard to tell how old the ruts were. One day? Three?

Will stretched, tired but knowing he wouldn't be able to sleep. The oxen were hobbled just beyond the orangish glow of the firelight. Will could hear them chewing their cuds. There were stands of pink flowering buckwheat all up and down the slopes ahead of them. The oxen wouldn't starve.

Will looked up at the stars and for the fiftieth time he clenched his fists and cursed his own stupidity. He had lost control of the team when he should have known how the smell of water would affect them. Here by the spring and as far as he could see beyond it, the ground was less rough. If they had been upwind of the spring, if the oxen had gone just a few hundred rods farther without bolting . . .

Will shook his head. It wasn't going to do any good to blame himself or the wind, or wish it hadn't happened. It had. Now, he had to think about what to do next.

As soon as there was light, Will got the map from his father's wallet and sat on a flat rock by the wagon, staring at the paper. If the map was accurate, they would emerge from this wash into a wider valley, then turn to head almost straight south.

"Will?"

He turned to see Jess coming toward him. Her

eyes were still puffy from sleep. "What are we going to do?"

Will showed her the map. "I'm going to go on ahead until I find help."

Jess was shaking her head. "No. We should stay together. Ma and I can figure out some way to move Pa. I was thinking last night that we could use the wagon cover to make a sling. Brownie and Becky are steady enough. . . ."

Will watched her eyes fill with tears. He cleared his throat and nodded. "You do that, Jess. And you explain to Ma where I've gone. When I get back with some help, we'll use the sling to get Pa out of here."

Jess touched his hand. "You can't go alone."

He squared his shoulders. "I can't see a choice, Jess. We can stay right here and starve in about three weeks. After we've killed all the oxen, there's no game. Or we can keep going, with Pa sick and feverish in a sling, and make three or four miles a day. Maybe there isn't enough graze for the oxen up ahead and they'd drop in their tracks. That'd mean we'd starve sooner."

"Don't talk like that, Will."

"It's just the truth, Jess. I have to find Tolford."

Jess was watching him wide-eyed. "I'm going with you, then."

Will shook his head. "And leave Ma without help?"

Jess stood up. "Ma will have water, and the boys can cut buckwheat for the oxen. What would happen if you twisted your ankle? What happens to all of us if you don't make it back?"

Will nodded slowly. There were no good choices left.

Chapter Nine

It scared Will to look at Pa. His skin was pale except for the fever flush across his cheeks. He had propped himself up on one elbow, and sweat beaded his forehead even though it was still chilly. The sun had been up only half an hour.

"I don't want either one of you to go," Ma said quietly. She had stopped crying, but her eyes were red and watery. Jess was sitting next to her, holding her hand.

"I can go alone," Will said.

"No." Jess shook her head. "It's too dangerous."

"I don't like it," Pa said. There was a tremor in his right arm and he shifted, trying to hide it.

"There's no choice," Will said. It was what he had

been saying from the beginning. He glanced at Eli and Jed. They were quiet, staring at Pa.

"It's not right for Jess to go," Pa said. "What if you meet Indians or—"

"But Eli is just too little," Jess broke in. "And Will can't go alone."

"Indians might help us," Will put in. "Or at least they'd show us where the springs are." He straightened up. "It's going to be hot in a couple of hours."

"It's out of the question as far as Jess is concerned," Ma began. "And Will—"

Pa cleared his throat, cutting her off. "They should go now, Mary," Pa said, and although his voice was shaky, it was clear he had made a decision. "We have no choice."

The next hour seemed like an eternity. Sweating and shaking, Pa copied the map. They filled both canteens and two stoppered vinegar bottles from Ma's kitchen box. Ma kept crying off and on and apologizing for her tears. Jess packed two canvas bags with blankets and spare clothes—a dress for her, and two shirts and a pair of trousers for Will. She put Pa's pistol in Will's bag, and a hunting knife in her own. Ma gave them nearly twenty pounds of dried meat, and Jess split it equally between them. Pa lay back through all the comings and goings and closed his eyes. Eli sat near him, and Jed puttered around the campfire, poking at the coals with a long stick.

Just as they were closing up their bags, Ma produced a tin of raisins she'd had hidden in her trunk. Will made her keep a handful each for Eli and Jed, then put the rest in two paper packets. He washed the tin and put the map in it, then slid it between the folds of his blanket. He hugged his little brothers, then stood back while Jess said her good-byes. Pa motioned him closer. Will knelt by the blanket bed.

"If I hadn't gotten hurt like this," Pa began.

"I know, Pa," Will said. "We'll be back as quick as we can."

"You're a good boy, Will," Pa told him. "You look out for your sister."

Will nodded, standing up again, scared by the sickly sheen of sweat on his father's brow, the stale smell that surrounded him. Ma was stiff-faced as he and Jess drank their fill from the spring. Then she began another round of good-byes.

By the time they finally set out, Will felt like he was dreaming. It was strange to walk away from his family. After a minute or two, they fell into a steady pace, with Will leading the way. Jess kept up without talking at all, lifting her skirts to step over the jagged rocks. Will glanced back and saw Ma waving—which made Jess look, too, and stumble. After that, he faced front again.

Will saw Tolford's tracks once or twice, then lost them again in the rocks. He waited until they had reached the bottom of the wash, passing from the rough, rocky land onto flat sand before he allowed himself to turn back one last time.

He frowned. They couldn't be more than a mile from camp, but some trick in the slope of the land now hid the wagon and Ma's blanket-and-sheet sunshade from view. Will heard Jess sigh and knew that it had caught her by surprise, too.

"We should see how far we can get before nightfall," Will said after a few seconds, trying to keep his voice even. He looked at the steep, broken slopes that rose to the west. "Up yonder is where we make the turn and head down the valley."

"Maybe we should find Tolford's wagon tracks first," Jess said. "What if he didn't turn south?"

Will looked across the mouth of the wash. It was no more than a half-mile wide. On either side, the hills were steep and rough. Tolford would have had no choice but to follow the route they had taken so far. But Jess was right. In front of them, looking up into what appeared to be a good-sized valley, he could see mountains to the west that had snow on them. Tolford might question the map. There was no telling what he might decide to do.

"We could just walk the wash from one side to the other," Jess suggested. "We're bound to come across the wheel tracks, aren't we?"

Will nodded. "I was just . . ." He hesitated. "I'm not Pa, Jess. I don't know what we should do."

"Sometimes, I think Pa just acts like he knows, even when he doesn't," Jess said quietly. She glanced up-slope, then turned toward him, a resolute expression on her face. "I'll go east and come back toward you if I don't find the tracks."

Uneasy at letting her go off alone, Will hesitated as she walked away. Then he turned abruptly and headed for the west side of the wash. After about fifty paces, he heard the raucous cawing of a raven and spun around, startled. The big black bird was sitting high on a boulder. It flew, something long and stringy dangling from its beak.

For an instant Will imagined a rattlesnake rising suddenly from a sandy burrow, striking. Then he pictured himself and Jess, both dead, their bodies dried up and wrinkled, lying beside the trail to frighten a family following a map much like their own. His bad luck and carelessness might mean the death of everyone he loved. He spit into the sand to chase the ugly thoughts away.

"Hey, Will!" Jess was waving her arms, signaling him. He started toward her.

They met halfway, and Jess pointed. "We'll run across the tracks if we go that way. I couldn't see far enough to tell if Tolford was turning south."

"I sure hope he does," Will said, feeling uneasy. If Tolford had gone north for some reason, their map would soon be useless.

Will let Jess set the pace. She seemed sturdy enough, but his own bag felt heavy, and he didn't want to wear her out. The sun was warm, but the air was still cool. They struck Tolford's tracks about a half mile from the wash and veered to follow them. The hard sand made easy going.

If they were lucky and kept up a good pace, they might be able to catch up with Tolford in a few days. The sun was fierce here—by noon it would be hot. Oxen pulling heavy wagons would travel even slower at midday. Will found himself whistling softly as they walked.

The country was strange. The mountains were gray, half barren, half angular, jutting rock. As the morning went by, the ground became bare stone in patches, with coarse sand in between. Pebbles were scattered over everything. It was hard for Will to keep his feet on the stone; the pebbles rolled beneath his weight. Jess was having trouble, too. The air was remarkably dry, and Will was thirsty within an hour even though it wasn't really hot out yet. He sipped at his canteen and saw Jess doing the same.

They kept on Tolford's trail, making their way through the sliding, grating rock. The country got bleaker by the mile. Odd shapes appeared in the outcroppings. Will stared up at a hillside that had eroded into ditches so close together they reminded him of plow furrows, except that some of them were several feet deep.

As they walked, Will shifted his bag from one

shoulder to the other, then back. The sky was clear, not a cloud to be seen. The sun blazed overhead, glazing the rock and sand, making him squint to shield his eyes from the painful brightness.

At noontime they stopped and ate a little dried meat. Jess had been sipping at her canteen all morning, but now she allowed herself a real drink. Will was quiet, which suited her fine. Her feet were hot, and she could feel a blister forming on her right heel. She was scared and tired and trying to stay hopeful. It felt good to stop walking, to rest. When Will stood up and asked if she was ready, she nodded reluctantly.

As they settled into a steady pace, Jess's bag was banging against the small of her back, in rhythm with her steps. She hitched it higher, amazed at how heavy it felt now. Starting off, it hadn't seemed so bad. She ignored the stinging on her skin where the strap rubbed, but knew she'd have to do something about it when they made camp for the night.

Jess began to wish Will would talk more. It was painful to keep imagining her father, feverish and sick, lying under a shelter that wouldn't keep out wind or cold. Eli and Jed would help Ma as much as they could, but they got tired and whiny.

Lost in her thoughts, not watching the ground, Jess slipped on some loose gravel and sat down hard. Will stopped and turned. "You all right?" He extended his hand.

Jess let him help her up, feeling foolish. "I was thinking about Ma and Pa. And the boys."

Will's face darkened. "Better not to. Just think about walking."

"I'm still hungry," Jess admitted.

Will nodded. "I am, too. But I think we should eat as little as we can. It has to last us, Jess."

Jess glanced past him at the wagon tracks that stretched from where they were standing into the distance, as far as she could see. "How long do you think it'll take us to catch up with Tolford?"

"How could I know?" Will exploded at her. "Stop asking me questions."

Jess stepped around him, furious. Wasn't it enough that they might die out here? That Pa was so sick? Will was acting like *she* had done something wrong. She raised her head high and kept walking, leading the way, not stopping to wait when she didn't hear his footsteps behind her. Finally, the crunch of gravel let her know he was coming. She refused to acknowledge him. He didn't apologize— or say anything else.

The sun was incredibly bright, and the air began to feel like an oven, still and dry. Jess's parched throat and bruised feet left little room for other thoughts. Sliding and stumbling, she struggled to make good time. She kept looking down the valley, hoping she would spot Tolford's wagons in the distance. But all she could see was more sand and rock.

The footing got worse. The gravel increased in size, and the ground beneath it hardened—until it was almost like walking on jagged ice. Jess had to fight to keep her balance, watching the ground intently, trying to place her feet. Will followed her without speaking, the only sound the clattering of loose stone.

Jess hitched her bag higher on her shoulder, struggling down an incline steep enough to make the rolling rock even more treacherous. Almost at the bottom, she slid sideways and nearly fell again. Will reached out to steady her, and she met his eyes for an instant.

"I'm sorry," he said as soon as she was on her feet.

She squeezed his hand before she released it. "It's all right."

Will squinted at the lowering sun. "Let's figure out where we're going to make camp."

"Does the map show a spring?"

Will nodded. "There's supposed to be another one. It's hard to say how much farther."

"I have enough water for tonight, and some in the morning, if I'm careful." Jess tried to sound matter-of-fact.

"I do, too," Will told her. He pointed at some over-hanging rocks a little ways off. "Maybe over there?"

Jess nodded and followed him when he led off. It was cooling off fast. In half an hour, she knew, she would be cold.

Chapter Ten

The morning dawned bright and sunny. Jess rolled free of her blanket and crawled out from under the rocky ledge. The crooked mesquite branch Will had used to check for snakes was still lying close by. He had covered his head with his blanket, and Jess could hear his deep, slow breathing. He was still sound asleep.

Jess stood looking up at the cloudless sky. The sand was cool beneath her bare feet. The sunshine was hot against her skin, and the air was already warming up. She swallowed. Her throat was sore, as though she had spent the day before shouting at the tops of her lungs. She looked down the valley. There were no wagons in sight.

Will stirred, and Jess watched him sit up, then took her canteen from her bag and tilted it to her lips. She meant to take a small drink, saving some water for later in the day. Instead, she downed two big gulps, then realized she had finished all but a spoonful. She reached into her bag and touched the cool glass of the vinegar bottle. It held less than half of what her canteen had held.

Jess glanced at Will. He was shaking sand from his socks and pulling them on. She found a flat rock to sit on and put on her own socks and shoes, picking a few barbed seeds from the knitted cotton. The water in her belly seemed to increase her hunger without really slaking her thirst.

She looked at Will. "Should we eat some of the raisins with our meat?" Will glanced at her, then shrugged, bending down to rummage through his bag. Jess felt a rush of anger so intense that it surprised her. "What's wrong with you? Why are you acting like all this is my fault?"

He stood up, glaring at her. He kicked at his bag. "I have about two swallows of water left in my canteen and I already ate half my raisins. Eat what you want. It isn't going to make any difference."

Jess stood. "Don't talk like that, Will."

He rubbed his hands over his face. "Why not? It's the truth."

"No, it isn't," she said, shaking her head. The fear that she barely had managed to suppress was rising. "It isn't true, it isn't," she heard herself repeating stupidly, her voice shrill. Then, helpless to prevent it, she began to cry.

"Leave off, Jess," Will was saying. "I already feel as bad as—"

"*You* feel bad?" Jess cut him off, wiping at her eyes. "What about Ma and Eli and Jed and—"

"It's my fault, Jess, not yours." Will interrupted her. "If I hadn't gone for the rifle and made Pa cut himself, none of this would have happened."

Jess stared at him. For the first time, the way Will had been acting began to make sense. "You can't believe that."

Will half-turned, looking out at the hills. "I should have held the oxen in, too. I should have thought about what the smell of water would do to them."

"And Pa should have thought about how hard all this would be on Ma and me and the boys. And you," she added fiercely. "Ma didn't want to leave Illinois.

And none of us wanted to leave the main wagon train. That was Pa's idea. Like taking this shortcut." She took a deep breath. "And I insisted on coming with you. I could have stayed by the spring with everyone else."

Will was shaking his head, but he was looking at her now. "Pa couldn't have known how bad this would be, Jess."

"And you couldn't have known how the oxen would react to the smell of water. And you never meant to hurt Pa."

Will dragged in a long breath, then let it out. "I should have held the team in."

"And I should have jumped down and run around in front of them. I thought about it. I was scared of falling on the rocks."

They both fell silent. Then Will cleared his throat. "The map shows a spring not too much farther south. Past a cliff, or a rock face. It rises up at the end of a wash."

Jess nodded at him, reaching into her bag. She pulled out her packet of raisins and offered him some. He took a few, then ruffled her hair, almost smiling. "You about ready, or do you have to starch your petticoats first?"

Jess laughed, pretending to curtsy. She hoisted her bag to her shoulder and had to bite her lip to keep from crying out. Her muscles were sore, but the raw skin where the strap had rubbed was by far more painful. She saw Will wince as he shouldered his bag, too, but he didn't complain.

By noon, Jess was almost dizzy with heat. They stopped and ate beneath a stand of mesquite trees, and she had to drink nearly half her water just to wash down the dried meat. It was all she could do to stand up and begin walking again. Will was quiet, but he rose from the spotty shade of the crooked trees and followed her. They walked side by side for a long time, following Tolford's tracks through the hot sand.

The afternoon passed slowly. Will was the first one to see the creek. He squeezed his eyes shut for a second. The glare of the sun on the sand made everything seem indistinct, blurry. He stared. There was some kind of plant, growing in a ragged line, and the glint of the sun on the water was unmistakable. It was real.

Turning clumsily to show Jess, he stumbled into

her and they both fell. Getting up, Will gestured, then panicked when he couldn't see the creek at first. There was sand all the way to the rugged mountains that rimmed the bowl of the valley. Wrenching around to help Jess to her feet, he nearly cried out in joy when he realized that he had just been facing the wrong way. The creek was still there.

He pointed again, and Jess smiled, ducking her head in pain as she touched her cracked lips. They gathered up their bags, Jess straightening her dirty bonnet. Leaving Tolford's tracks, Will kept his eyes on the shine of the water.

As they got closer, he could see an odd blurring, a strange lightness around the creek itself. That thought barely had time to pass before another barged into his mind. White. The ground around the creek was white? They kept walking.

"Salt." Jess's voice was flat.

Will wanted to argue with her, prayed that she was wrong. But he knew she wasn't.

"All of this is salt," Jess said sadly as they came up to the edge of the sluggish creek.

Will's shoes crunched over the dirty white crust that got thicker and thicker, coating the muddy sand beside the stream. He bent to cup a handful of the water. It smelled bad. "Don't drink it," he warned Jess as she reached down.

He watched her wet her hand, then raise it to her nose. She made a sound of disgust. "It stinks." She looked at the sky. "How can it be salt?" she demanded. "How can it just be . . . salt?" Her voice was shrill.

"Take it easy, Jess," Will said.

Suddenly, she stepped back from the bank, pulled her shoes off and set them on a rock. Lifting her skirt, she waded into the creek.

"Maybe it's poison," Will said.

Jess shrugged, swaying on her feet. "Grandma Tate used to soak her bunions in salt water."

Will sat down on the rock where she had left her shoes. "You don't know whether it's just salt. It smells strange."

Reluctantly, Jess waded out. She picked up her shoes, and Will looked down at her feet. They were clotted with mud and the clinging white salt.

He shrugged. "The mud will come off as it dries. We only have an hour or so before dark, Jess." Will meant to stand up as he said it, but he only glanced at the endless blue sky, then back at his sister. He licked his lips. The sound of the trickling creek made him thirstier than ever. But there were only a few swallows left in his vinegar bottle, and he was pretty sure Jess had even less. "This isn't the spring on the map," he said.

Jess nodded. "I know. How much farther, do you think?"

Will could tell she was struggling to stay calm, and he reached down into his bag to pull out the map Pa had drawn. He set the tin aside and spread the paper on the rock. Jess moved her shoes to sit beside him.

"It doesn't even show this creek," Jess murmured, turning the map toward herself.

"It only shows the good water," Will told her. "I think, anyway," he added.

Jess sagged forward and rested her head on his shoulder. Then she straightened up. "We shouldn't stay here any longer." She began scuffing her feet in the sand, rubbing the mud off.

Will nodded, but it still took a minute before he could pick up his bag and get to his feet. He shot a look of hatred toward the salt creek. The water looked clear and good and it sounded cool and . . .

"We should go," Jess said, interrupting his thoughts.

She was refastening her shoes. "We can't stop, Will."

He nodded, knowing in some inner part of his mind that they sounded like five-year-olds, repeating everything two or three times. He smiled, meaning to share the joke with Jess. The sudden pain from his cracked lips made the smile disappear, and an instant later, he couldn't recall what the joke had been. Mr. Tolford had been right. Being thirsty long enough made people stupid.

Will swung back into a stiff-kneed walk, his sister beside him. The sand was white in long stretches now, the salt crust marked by the deep wheel ruts from Tolford's wagons.

Near dusk, they came upon a flock of ravens at the base of a rocky cliff. The big black birds were swarming over the carcass of an ox. One of Tolford's? It had to be. Will stopped a dozen feet away and lifted his arms, trying to startle them. A few took wing, but only circled and came back.

"Leave them alone," Jess whispered. Then she cleared her throat. "I'm tired, Will."

He nodded, watching as one of the ravens picked at the ox's closed eye.

"Will!"

He turned to face her. She was standing with her hands on her hips, her bag resting on top of her feet. She was swaying slightly. He forced himself to look around, trying to clear his thoughts. They should find shelter of some kind. He tried to spot trees or a rock outcropping, or even a wash that would hide them, but there was nothing but flat land. Up ahead, he could see broken hills and rough, dry country stretching to the mountains on either side.

His eyes clung to the western peaks for a long moment. They were covered with white, and up that high, it would not be the false, cruel promise of salt. He imagined the cold, wet feeling of snow in his mouth.

"Will?"

He tried to swallow and found he couldn't. His throat was so dry that it stuck closed, and he had to cough. A stand of brush on a high point caught his attention. He gestured. Jess nodded and started off, taking unsteady little steps, her bag swinging against her back.

An hour later, Will sat beside the fire they had made. They had divided the water evenly and finished every drop. They had nothing to cook, nothing to eat but dried meat and the last few of Jess's raisins to share. Eating the meat was a monumental chore—it felt like wads of old rags in his dry mouth. He kept chewing, trying to choke it down, but it was almost impossible. They had passed the cliffs shown on the map, hadn't they? So they would probably come across the spring in the morning.

"There's a fire," Jess said quietly, and for a moment, Will thought she was talking nonsense.

"Of course there is," he said. "You helped me build it."

"No." She was tugging at him, leaning her weight back to make him stand up. She pulled him a few steps away, pointing, breathless.

He started to argue with her, but then he saw it, too. There. In the distance was a tiny, flickering fire, the size of an orange star in the darkness of the night.

"Tolford?" Jess murmured.

"Or Indians," Will answered. He stared at the little fire. It was so far away. Maybe too far.

Chapter Eleven

Sunup woke them both. Jess lay still in her blanket, rubbing her aching eyes. There were no clouds, not even a wisp of white in the sky. She stretched and winced at the pain in her back and shoulders. Her feet ached, too. Her belly was empty again, but what she felt wasn't exactly hunger. All her aches and pains were blurred, too. Her thirst eclipsed everything else. Until she could find water, enough water to really drink deep, nothing else would matter very much.

"Except finding Tolford," she whispered to herself, frightened that she had forgotten for an instant.

"What?" Will rasped.

Jess cleared her throat. "We can't waste daylight." She reached for her bonnet.

Will groaned. "I know, I know." He rolled to a sitting position, then rocked forward onto his knees. Jess caught a flash of movement that jangled at her sense of reality. Will's blanket was moving, as if he was wriggling his toes—but he was kneeling. His toes were behind him.

The blanket moved again, and Jess pointed, mute, unable to say anything aloud. Will frowned at her, obviously confused. An instant later, the fold nearest the ground widened, and Jess caught a glimpse of something sliding inside it. The brownish color, the scaled-slick skin—

"Snake," she managed. "In your blanket, Will. A snake!"

He looked puzzled for a split second longer, then flung the blanket away, jumping to his feet and staggering backward. Jess leaped up, lurching to one side. The rattler slid from beneath the mounded blanket. It moved oddly, like no snake Jess had ever seen before. It crawled sideways, flowing across the slope, picketing the sand with parallel marks. It was shaking its tail, its stone eyes fixed on her face. This was a sidewinder, she was sure.

"Get away from it! "Will rasped. Out of the corner

of her eye, Jess saw him stumble over his own feet, then catch his balance again. The snake slowed, turning to look at Will, then again to face her. She took a step backward, waving her bonnet—and the snake moved toward her again.

"Jess!" Will was frantic now. "If you can get it far enough from the bag, I can get Pa's pistol."

Jess nodded without taking her eyes off the sidewinder. If she moved too fast, it would likely head for the shelter of the blanket again, or even crawl into Will's open bag. They might have to wait all day for it to crawl out—Jess tried to think of another way to get it out without getting bitten. She couldn't.

When the snake was about ten feet from her, Jess stepped back once more, bending forward to scoop up a little sand in her free hand, then straightening quickly. The snake had not pursued her this time. She flung the sand at it, peppering its head. It rattled louder, its tail vibrating with fear and fury.

"Come on," Jess whispered. But the snake held its ground, then turned to look at Will once more. "As soon as I get it to move toward me," Jess said to Will without looking at him, "you start toward the bag."

"All right," Will said hoarsely.

Barely moving her hand, Jess swung her bonnet back and forth. The snake stared at it, sliding forward, its neck arched menacingly. Jess waited for a second longer than she wanted to, then stepped back again, glancing behind herself to make sure she wouldn't stumble over anything.

"Jess!"

Will's shout startled her. She stared at the snake, not five feet from her leg now. Without thinking, she flung her bonnet at it and sprang backward as it struck. Confused by the cloth, it missed, but Jess's feet tangled in her skirts and she sprawled onto the sand.

The sidewinder had stopped. Jess stared at it. From this angle, with her face against the sand, the snake seemed closer, impossibly knotted, its slick scales hissing on the sand as it coiled tighter. Its ribbon tongue flickered in and out of its mouth.

"Don't move," Will was saying. "Don't move at all, Jess."

Jess almost nodded, then realized even that could be fatal. The sidewinder was arched at attention, its head high, only an arm's length up the slope from her. Her bonnet lay to one side, soiled and forlorn.

"I'll shoot on three." Jess could hear Will's voice shaking.

Jess waited. Every grain of sand between her and the snake was a distinct and separate shape. A tiny beetle crawled past, and she could see eyelash-fine hairs on its legs.

"One."

Jess wanted to close her eyes, to shut out the tense curves of the snake's body.

"Two."

Will's voice seemed far away. Everything seemed distant except the heat of the sand on her cheek and the blunt, wedged head of the sidewinder.

"Three."

The sound of the shot shattered Jess's small world, enlarging it again. In a spasm of reflexes, she rolled, seeing the sky, then the sand, then the blue arch overhead once more. Will shouted something, but she couldn't understand him. She heard a second shot and felt sand spatter her legs. She convulsed at the stinging touch, scrambled to her feet, and ran a few steps, then danced back around to face her brother.

The snake lay in front of him, still writhing, its head nearly severed from its body. Her bonnet was spattered with red and gray. Pa's pistol dangled from Will's hand.

He looked up. "Are you all right?"

Jess brushed at her skirt and tried to still the shaking in her hands. "Yes." Her voice was so tight, it sounded like a frog's croak. She cleared her throat and repeated it. "Yes."

Will reloaded the pistol and dropped it back in his bag. Then he sat down and slouched forward. "We have to find water," he said suddenly. "Jess, we just have to."

She nodded, then realized he wasn't looking at her anymore. He was watching the dead snake again as it writhed in the sand. "The map says we're close," she said, trying to keep her voice steady. Her knee-caps jerked and jumped, and her legs were still quivering. She wanted to get away from the snake, to stop watching its death throes.

She went to stand beside Will, walking a wide circle around the snake. She squeezed his shoulder, and he reached up to take her hand for a few seconds. Then he shambled to his feet and closed up his bag. Jess watched him, his movements like an old man. He was right. They had to find water—and they had to find it soon.

Will saw the glaring sand in front of him through a haze of pain. There was a throbbing pulse in his head that seemed to radiate from the center of his brain outward. The backs of his eyes ached, beating in unison with his swollen feet. He kept glancing back at Jess. Her head was down, and she shuffled along steadily without complaining, her bag slung low on her back.

There was no shade, only the ever-widening salt deposits that covered the valley floor. The sunlight sparkled and danced on the dirty, whitish surface, and Will rubbed at his sore eyes, trying to clear his vision. To the east was a distant glimmer that looked like a huge lake. That was impossible, wasn't it? Maybe it was just more salt.

"Will?"

He stopped, and Jess bumped into him from behind. For a moment, they struggled to keep their feet, gripping each other's forearms in a clumsy circular waltz.

"The map?" Jess asked in a paper-dry voice.

Will let go of her, straightening a little to let his bag slide to the ground. He knelt heavily and undid the straps. The buckles seemed smaller, harder to grip than they had before. He managed the first two, then stared at the third, unable for a few seconds to make himself start over. Once he had it free, he glanced up at Jess, startled to find her bending over him, her face only a few inches from his own.

"The map?" She grimaced, rubbing at her eyes. "Shouldn't we look at the map?"

Will began to search through his bag. His blanket tangled beneath his hands, and he shoved it to one side, uncovering the empty canteen and the vinegar bottle that lay beside it. He looked at them with a painful longing that completely displaced every other thought and concern. For a long moment all he knew was that he wanted water. He wanted water to drink, to wade, to immerse himself in. He was suddenly overcome by a memory of the farm pond at home. The image was so beautiful that he could only turn toward his sister. "Remember the pond?"

Jess nodded, and a look of pain contorted her features. "The map, Will. Find the map."

He nodded again and went back to rifling through his bag. The paper was at the bottom, inside Ma's old cookie tin, exactly where he had put it. He lifted it out and rocked back on his heels, sitting in the scalding sand, spreading the paper out before him.

Jess dropped to the sand beside him. "Where are we now?"

Will jabbed a finger at the paper. "Here somewhere. I think."

Jess peered at the map. "There's the cliff," she said slowly, deliberately.

Will nodded, trying to focus. He glanced up, slitting his eyes against the morning sun, then turning his head to the right to face southward. The salt-covered sand went on forever. There were scattered clumps of reeds or tule rushes, but no mesquite or greasewood trees. The salt glimmered and shone—it'd be impossible to tell salt from water at any distance.

"Look at this," Jess whispered.

Will looked down at paper flattened over the hot sand. She was pointing at a rough circle that Pa had labeled BADWATER SUMP. The spring was marked just northwest of it. "We haven't passed anything like that, have we?" she asked, looking up at him.

"I saw something to the southeast." He pointed.

Jess stood up and looked. "I see it, I think. A shine? Like more salt water?"

Will shrugged. "Could be."

"Then we have to be close to the spring, Will." Her voice faded from a rasp back into a whisper. Will stared at her reddened face and noticed for the first time that she wasn't wearing her bonnet. Had she lost it? Before he could ask, she was pulling at her skirts, trying to stand up.

He put the map into its tin and closed it. He fastened two of the straps on his bag, then gave up on the third and stood up quickly. Too quickly. By the time his dizziness eased, Jess was already a little ways ahead. He began walking, his eyes fixed on her back.

The sand smoothed out as they went, the surface becoming so flat that the sun-glare worsened. Will found himself looking at the mountains to the west, or all the way across the glittering salt in the valley to the hills on the other side, trying to ease his eyes. The soft, crunching sound of Jess's footsteps blended with his own and became a peaceful backdrop for his spinning thoughts.

When the odd, sharp sound intruded, it made no

sense to Will at first. Jess did not turn, or slow, and he wondered if he was imagining it. It was familiar, and it tugged at him like a memory, pulling him to a stop. He tried to call out to Jess, but she could not hear his hoarse whisper and he could not seem to make his voice any louder.

The sound came again and again. It was not too far away, Will was sure. He turned ponderously, searching the shining white surface of the salt flats. There. The sound was coming from a thin scattering of tule a little ways to the west. And now he knew what it was. There were ducks behind the reeds.

Without thinking further, Will fumbled at his bag, undoing one strap, then reaching through the flap and feeling for the pistol. He pulled it out, dropping one bullet in the sand before he managed to load it, then straightened and began a long, strided, stiff-legged walk toward the reeds.

Jess had not looked back, and Will thought about shouting, then remembered that he already had tried once and had not been able to do it. His attention fastened itself on the tule rushes, and he lifted the pistol, sighting along the barrel as his father had taught him. He shuffled closer, his mind still except for the thought that Pa would be proud of him if he could kill a duck for supper.

Will squeezed his eyes shut, then opened them wide. When the ducks heard him and startled into flight, he automatically swung with them and led his shot, aiming just a little ahead so the bullet would meet the duck in flight. Slowly, smoothly, he pulled the trigger. He saw the duck jerk to one side and drop. A little explosion of feathers told him his shot had been true.

He croaked a painful cheer and shot once more, straight up into the air. It was only then that he heard Jess's rough shout, demanding to know what was wrong. He stumbled toward her, then veered off, remembering the duck. Pa would never approve of leaving it in the water this long.

The thought resonated in his sluggish mind, and he worked at it, trying to understand. Would water hurt a duck? He chuckled. At the edge of the tules, he slid the pistol into his pocket and then went on, scanning the surface of the narrow marsh.

He was three steps into the water before he realized it was there. Once he did, he fell to his knees, sobbing.

Chapter Twelve

Jess couldn't stop drinking. The water was warm, but it tasted sweet and it soothed the raw and swollen lining of her throat. She splashed her face, soaking the front of her dress, noticing the mud as she knelt, then forgetting it as she began to drink once more. She could hear Will's sobs broken by the sound of coughing, and she knew she should go to him, but she was helpless to do anything but try to assuage her clawing thirst. The water was so delicious.

The first wave of nausea startled Jess and rocked her back on her heels. The searing sun pressed down on her, and she stood, half-turning, her hand clasped against her belly. The too-bright sand began to spin beneath her feet.

She sank to her knees again. A groaning sound came from her lips, followed by a desperate rush of water spewing from her mouth, gagging her with its cloying warmth. She vomited over and over, gasping for breath in the seconds when the heaving stopped, retching hard when it began again. She could hear Will throwing up, too. Was the water poison?

Finally, the retching stopped, and she lay exhausted on her back, dragging in deep breaths, the piercing sun in her eyes. She wasn't sure how long she had been lying there or where Will had gone. She called his name, her throat so raw that her voice was barely audible. There was no answer.

Rolling onto her side, Jess felt the nausea rise again and she gagged, but there was nothing left to come up. She waited until she could lift her head, then tried to see her brother. She spotted his bag first, lying not far from her own, both coated with salt dust and grimy sand.

She got to her knees, then managed to stand, trying to call to him, her voice a ragged whisper. Fighting for her balance with every step, her skirts tripping her, Jess waded the shallows past the first uneven line of tule rushes.

Will was on his back in the shallow water, his face and shoulders propped above the surface by a hummock of tule rushes. His eyes were open, but dull, and for a terrifying second, Jess thought he was dead. Falling to her knees beside him, she pounded at his chest with her fists. He began to cough again, and she hauled him onto his side, rolling him half across her lap as he choked and gagged.

Once Will was breathing steadily again, Jess collapsed, resting her cheek on his shoulder, staring sideways at the muddied water around them. Her thirst was returning, and she knew it wouldn't be long before she would want to drink again. The idea frightened her.

Will stirred, and she straightened to let him sit up. His face was the color of chalk. He looked at her, then wiped futilely at the mud on her dress front, shaking his head.

"We have to drink slower," he said as if he were talking to himself. "It's like . . . foundering."

Jess reached up to push his wet hair back from his eyes. Of course. No one she knew was stupid enough to let an overheated horse or mule drink its fill of water all at once. How could they have been so foolish?

Jess sat still, letting her stomach settle, trying to calm herself. It was logical and obvious. They had vomited up the water because they'd foundered themselves, that was all. The water wasn't poison.

Will had moved a few feet away from her, still on his knees, sloshing in the shallows. He reached down and picked up something that swung loosely from his hand. Jess recognized the slick feathers of a duck. Will turned toward her, raising it, smiling wanly. He waded out, and sat down heavily beside their bags.

Jess struggled to stand up, her soaked skirts clinging to her legs. She stepped out of the water, clumsy and off balance. She walked along the edge until she found a place they had not muddied. Forcing herself to swallow only twice, she took another drink. Then, resolutely, she stood up again and went to sink onto the sand beside her brother.

"Are you all right?" he asked after a moment.

Jess nodded. "I think so." She shivered as a stray breeze cooled her wet dress. After a time, she felt her thoughts were finally her own again—not just disjointed words that came and went as they pleased.

Will pointed at the duck. "As soon as I can do it without hurting myself, I'll clean this and we can—"

"Don't talk about food yet," Jess interrupted him, feeling her stomach tighten.

He set the duck on the sand behind his bag, and Jess was grateful. The bloody patch just behind its wing was making her feel incredibly sad. It could have flown away, out of this awful place forever. Now it was dead. Another breath of wind passed and made the wet cloth that stuck to her legs feel clammy against her skin. She glanced up at the sky. There was a bank of clouds lying along the tops of the peaks to the west. How long had it been there?

Will crawled to the edge of the water, and Jess could hear him drinking. Cautious, she waited until he had finished, then couldn't resist any longer. She knelt at the water's edge and drank again, allowing herself three swallows this time. The water still tasted like heaven.

Jess licked her lips, noticing for the first time how crusted the corners of her mouth were. There was a thick coating on the inside of her lower lip, too. Disgusted, she bent over the water and scrubbed at her face.

When she straightened, the heavy wetness of her dress hobbled her, nearly making her lose her balance. While Will began to scoop out a fire pit in the sand, Jess dragged her bag behind him and managed to peel off her wet clothing, sliding on her extra dress. It was tight across the shoulders, but she didn't care. Even though her head ached and her muscles were still cramping and her belly lay uneasily inside her, the clean, dry cloth felt wonderful. She rinsed out her muddy clothes and draped them across some tules to dry.

Jess looked around, spotting a stand of mesquite not too far away. She glanced back at Will. He was tugging at the straps on his bag. She went to help him. The straps were stiff, and Jess opened one while Will managed the other. He pulled out a clean shirt and trousers. His face was still too white, but his eyes were alive again, and when she spoke his name, he looked up.

"I'll get some mesquite wood for a fire," Jess said. Her throat was still raw and sore. She waited until he looked at her. "We can't go any farther today, can we?"

"I can't." Will shook his head. "I really thought we were going to die."

"I did, too," Jess admitted. *And we still might*, she thought, but didn't allow herself to say it aloud. Will was probably thinking exactly the same thing, but if he wasn't, she didn't want to discourage him. He was so pale. She wondered if her own skin was as white. If it was, this was the only time in her life she'd ever have a proper lady's complexion, she was sure.

Heaving herself to her feet, Jess turned toward the mesquite trees. She walked slowly across the hot sand. Her shoes were wet, and the grit had worked its way inside to cake her ankles. With every step, her body ached to lie down, but at least the knife-blade sharpness of her thirst had been dulled now.

The first scattered mesquite trees that she came to were thick-trunked and gnarled. Near the roots of one of the largest, Jess saw a scooped-out den. She slowed her step to peer into it. Coyotes? It almost looked too big. The shadowy interior kept her from judging how far back the animals had dug. She shook her head, chiding herself for wasting time, and turned back toward the thickest part of the mesquite.

For the first time in a long time, her thoughts drifted to her family. Was Pa all right? He had prob-ably either recovered, or the fever had killed him by now. She swallowed hard, refusing to cry. Ma didn't need tears. She and the boys needed help.

"We'll find Tolford in the morning," Jess whispered to herself as she broke a crooked limb and laid it on the sand. "We saw his fire. It won't be too much longer."

She stood, looking for deadwood. A low limb caught her eye. The wood was brittle, lifeless. She ducked beneath it, straightening slowly, freeing her hair when it snagged in the short, crooked twigs. She leaned on the dead limb, bouncing her weight against it. It held. She released it and stood back.

She had to get some bigger limbs. If she managed only twigs and kindling, it was going to be nearly impossible to cook the duck—and they had to eat. They had to be strong enough to get up in the morning and walk fast enough to catch up to Mr. Tolford.

Jess repositioned herself farther out along the branch. Stiff-armed, she shoved downward, then pulled the limb as far as she could sideways. Breathing hard, her efforts ponderous and clumsy, she worked at flexing it upward, then down, then to both sides. It became a slow-tempoed repetition that carried her beyond her own thoughts again. When the wood finally cracked and broke, she sank to the ground with it.

Jess wasn't sure how long it had taken for her to gather the wood, but by the time she staggered back to the spring, dragging the biggest limbs behind herself, Will was sitting up, wearing clean clothes. His wet clothes were hanging on the rushes near hers. The duck, gutted and skinned, lay on a pile of tule rushes beside the fire pit. Will looked up at Jess when she came close.

"I was going to come help you, but I got so dizzy. . . ."

"I made out all right," Jess assured him, trying to keep the tremor of fatigue out of her own voice. She dropped the wood and managed to walk three steps from it before she stumbled. On her hands and knees, she crawled the rest of the way to the water's edge and drank again.

"I can't stop, either," Will told her when she turned and sat, facing him. "I was going to bring you that." He pointed, and Jess saw that he had filled her canteen. "I couldn't carry it, Jess." He sounded so sad.

"We'll be stronger tomorrow," Jess said, nodding

as though she were agreeing with something he had said. She tried to smile at him.

"Do you suppose Ma and Pa—"

"They're probably fine," Jess cut him off. "They have the oxen for meat and a good spring."

Will seemed to accept that, and Jess was grateful. Her own fear for their family was far too close to the surface to stand much discussion. She leaned forward, reaching to pull his bag closer. The matches were in their waxed box, beneath his blanket. She fumbled it open and spilled them onto the sand. Furious with herself, Jess picked them up one by one, careful not to lose any.

"I'll start the fire," she said slowly. "Is there a piece long and straight enough to use as a spit?"

He nodded and turned away without saying anything. She watched him for a few seconds, worried. He was better, but he seemed so weak, so exhausted. It wasn't like Will to let things defeat him like this. If he lost his good spirits completely, she wasn't at all sure she could hold on to her own. She felt like crying, like burying her face in Ma's apron. Resolutely shoving the thought aside, she placed the matches by the fire pit and stood up.

◊ ◊ ◊

Will glanced at Jess and realized she was staring at him. He looked away. He didn't want her to see how little hope he had. Even more than that, he didn't want to admit why. His father's pistol was somewhere in the mud. Whatever their chances had been, he had made them much worse.

Will stood slowly and turned toward the wood Jess had dragged back. There was more than enough to cook the duck, he was pretty sure. He picked out a slender branch and broke off a two-foot length that was fairly straight. Then he braced one foot against another branch and reached down to pull the end upward. It snapped, and he tossed it aside, shifting his attention to the next piece.

By the time he had broken the wood as well as he was able to, Jess was on her way back. He sat, shading his eyes from the cruel light of the sun, watching her. She walked so slowly that he could tell it had cost most of her strength to gather the dried moss he could see dangling from her right hand. Her head was down, and she only glanced up now and then to change her direction slightly as she made her way toward him.

"This'll make tinder, I think," she said as she got closer. She stopped at the edge of the water to drink, and he found himself struggling back to his feet to go kneel beside her. The water tasted almost as good this time as it had at first.

"The wagon tracks are right over there," Jess said as they straightened up.

"What?" Will looked at her, not understanding.

"Tolford's wagons. They stopped here."

Will shook his head. "How did we miss them?"

Jess shrugged. "My mind still doesn't feel right. We could have walked straight past Chicago and I wouldn't have noticed."

Will nodded, meeting her eyes. "I lost the pistol, Jess."

"You lost . . ." Her voice was soft, not accusing, but he could see some of the hope that had begun to reappear in her eyes wink out.

Chapter Thirteen

Will woke at dawn and lay very still as his dreams faded and reality solidified. A swirling rill of wind kicked up sand that spattered his face. He turned his head.

"I wish we could stay here another day," Jess said suddenly, startling him.

He looked at her. Her skin was bright red from sunburn. "We can't, Jess. The earlier we leave, the better."

"I know." Jess pushed her blanket down and sat up.

Another sudden gust of wind flipped the corner of her blanket over and made Will squint against the sting of blown sand. Jess was already on her way to the water's edge. Will stood up slowly, letting his blanket fall and stepping over it.

The water was cooler from the night air. He drank like a horse at a trough, sucking up huge swallows and gulping them down. When he finally sat back, he found Jess watching him.

"Do you feel better this morning?"

He shrugged. "Sure. But I still get sick every time I think about Pa's pistol somewhere out there in all that mud."

Jess looked out across the narrow marsh. "We could look again. . . ."

Will shook his head. "I looked for a long time, Jess. It's buried in the mud. Even if we found it now, it'd probably be useless."

Jess frowned, running her hand through her tangled hair. "Tolford can't be too far ahead of us, can he? If his oxen are dying, he'll have to slow down."

Will heard a whistling sound and looked past her without answering. The wind was rising. There was a whitish haze above the mountains to the east. Looking up the valley, back the way they had come, the air seemed brownish and dirty.

"Is that smoke?" Jess asked.

Will shrugged. "I don't think so. The wind is just kicking up the dust, I guess."

"That high?" Jess was craning her head to see the mountain tops to the west.

Will scanned the horizons. There was a dusty brown tinge to the air in every direction. He pushed his hair back off his forehead. The wind was picking up sharply, but the sky straight overhead was clear blue.

Jess suddenly scrambled to her feet. Will jumped up, whirling, afraid she had seen another snake. But she was pointing upward at an angle, her eyes wide as she stared. He followed her gesture. At first he saw nothing, then a flickering shape caught his eye. There, in the distance, was an elongated smudge of brown, hanging in the air above the valley.

"What is that?" Jess breathed.

Will didn't answer her. He squinted, trying to focus on the elusive shape. It darkened, then lightened again.

Jess tugged his sleeve. "Remember what Mr. Bailey said about the Paiute air spirits?"

Will glanced down at her. "That's just stories, Jess."

She looked back at the flickering shape. "You don't know that. Will, there's no storm, no clouds, no lightning at all. It can't just be a cyclone, it's . . ." She trailed off.

Will watched the shape darken again. This time it stayed clearly visible, a slender, curving line that connected the sand to the sky. The base seemed to widen a little as it came toward them.

"It *is* a cyclone," Jess cried out, dragging at his arm. "It is, Will, we have to run!"

Tearing his eyes from the bizarre wind funnel, Will let her pull him along, glancing over his shoulder as often as he could. The funnel was growing, and it was coming toward them. It swayed, sagging under the weight of the sand inside it. Over the sound of their footsteps, Will could hear a hissing sound that got louder and louder.

Jess stumbled, falling hard, and Will had to jump over her to keep from hurting her. He spun around and was astonished to see the strange sand-colored cyclone so close that he could pick out a ragged branch, whirling inside it.

As Jess got up, Will pulled her forward and got her running again. He headed almost straight westward, taking a cross-path like Pa had always told them to do.

"Will!" Jess was pulling him to stop, gesturing wildly.

He turned. The funnel was lightening in color

and rising, no longer connected to the ground. As Will watched, his heart pounding, it leaped skyward, glimmered above their heads, then disappeared. There was no falling sand, no cloud of dust spreading out above, nothing. It was simply gone. No one who had not seen it a moment before would ever believe that it had existed at all.

Will could hear the beating of his heart. Jess's breathing was quick and light like a cornered rabbit's. He shook his head and tried to laugh. "I guess here in California they don't have to have a thunderstorm to have a cyclone."

Jess glared up at the blue sky. "I hate this place." The wind gusted and blew her hair across her eyes. She swiped at it angrily. "I do. I hate California. I wish we had never left home."

Will could hear a tremor in her voice, and her eyes were shiny with tears. He reached out to take her hand, and she snatched it away. "I wanted to stay in Illinois. I just wanted . . . ," she began, and he could tell she was trying not to cry.

"We have to pack up and get moving," Will said. "We stand a chance of finding Tolford today if we can make good time."

He watched her swipe at her eyes, nodding.

She turned on her heel and started toward the spring. Her back was straight, and her head was high. She didn't walk fast, but her pace was steady and Will just watched her for a second, admiring her gumption. Then he made himself walk fast enough to catch up with her. It wasn't easy. Every muscle in his body seemed to be tired and sore.

The wind strengthened as Jess folded their clean clothes and put their bags in order. Will filled their canteens and the vinegar bottles with fresh water. By the time Jess was through washing her hands and face, the gusts were strong enough to blow stinging sand around her ankles. Will was still bent over the water, scrubbing at his face with open palms.

Jess looked longingly at the narrow marsh formed by the spring. She didn't want to leave it. She was afraid to. If they didn't find Tolford today, they would soon be as thirsty and dull-witted as they had been before. Her throat was still raw and sore. She remembered the raking pain of the thirst, and it made her shudder.

"You ready?" Will asked her as he got to his feet.

She nodded, knowing that if she said anything at all he would hear how frightened she was. She was an inch away from crying again, and that would be pure foolishness. They had no time to lose.

Will shouldered his bag and led off, swinging westward to pick up Tolford's wagon tracks. Jess followed, wadding up her spare dress and pushing it beneath the strap to pad her shoulder. The stinging pain lessened immediately, and she wished she had thought of it earlier.

The wind swirled her skirts, gusting to plaster the cloth against the backs of her legs, then dropping again. Overhead, the air had taken on a strange pearly whiteness, and the sun, still not far above the horizon, was a reddish-brown disk. Its light rouged everything slightly, making the sand unfamiliar and eerie-looking. Jess looked around for another funnel. The sky was still cloudless except for the blowing dust, but that hadn't mattered before.

"You all right?"

Will's voice made her realize she was falling behind. With the wind shoving at her, she shuffled a few steps to catch up. The next gust slapped her hair across her face, and she longed for her bonnet.

"Come on, Jess."

She nodded, and they set off again. She hurried, but it was hard to match Will's long-legged strides. She was so tired. As the wind rushed past them, it seemed to blow her back and forth like a blade of grass. It was getting stronger.

After a few minutes, the driven sand that had been racing along the ground seemed to rise, stinging through her skirts and bodice. Her extra dress slipped from beneath the strap, and she struggled to tuck it into place without slowing her step. Will was walking with his head down now, not glancing back. Jess understood why. The onslaught of the blown sand was more fierce by the second.

Jess lowered her own head, her chin almost resting on her chest. She narrowed her eyes. She could still see well enough to follow Tolford's tracks, the deep ruts a clear marker in the sand. The sound of the wind had risen to a whining roar, a frightening sound. She risked a glance upward and saw the sky overhead had turned the color of dust. The sun was now a muddy disk that wavered and shifted.

A sudden blast of wind drove sand into Jess's half-turned cheek. The pain was sharp, and she instinctively reached up to protect her face, turning out of the wind. She ducked her head again and ran a step or two to catch up with Will. Eyes nearly shut, she felt a strange coolness on her cheek and touched it once more. When she lowered her hand, she saw that her fingertips were bloody.

Jess looked at the ground again. She coughed, choking on the dust, and glanced up just in time to keep from walking straight into Will. He had stopped.

"Tolford's tracks," Will shouted at her over his shoulder.

Jess stared, not understanding for a few seconds. Then, she understood all too well. The sand was shifting under the wind. It wasn't just the rills of lacy wind-driven grit now. The floor of the desert was being swept. Tolford's tracks were rapidly filling in, disappearing.

Desperate, Jess spun to face the wind, trying to see the marsh around the spring behind them. They hadn't come that far, had they? A swirling cloud of dense dust and sand came roaring toward her. She whipped around, letting her bag drop as she covered her face in her arms.

"We have to find shelter," she screamed at Will.

"Where?" he screamed back. "Maybe if we just lie down—"

"No!" Jess pictured the choking sand covering them, suffocating them. There had to be something they could do, somewhere they could hide from the wind. Abruptly, she remembered the coyote den. It had looked abandoned. She hadn't seen tracks around it, had she? But they had no pistol, no weapon. Would coyotes attack them?

Will was nearly bent double. "Maybe we should try to get back to the spring."

Jess shouted agreement and picked up her bag as they turned to face the terrible wind.

It was almost impossible. The sand was like tiny razors, cutting at any patch of unprotected skin. Jess sagged to her knees, crying out. Will stopped and came toward her. He pulled his spare shirts out of his bag. Wrestling the madly fluttering cloth, they managed to tie makeshift turbans around their heads, the sleeves crossing over their cheeks and secured around their necks.

As they got closer to the spring, Jess agonized over whether to lead Will toward the barely visible stand of mesquite. If there were coyotes . . . Then the wind made her decision for her. It shifted so quickly, roaring with a sudden surge of fury, that they were both knocked off their feet.

"Over there! I saw a coyote den when I got firewood!" Jess shouted, close to Will's ear. Without giving him time to argue or even question her, she veered eastward, crawling until they could stand.

As hard as it had been to walk straight into the wind, walking at an angle to it was even harder. Jess fell again and could not have risen without Will's help. Leaning against each other, shoulders braced, legs slanting outward, they staggered onward.

The mesquite trees were bent before the wind, and nothing looked familiar to Jess. She could barely see, peering through tiny slits in the cloth that covered her face. When she finally saw the coyote den, she knew that it was luck or Providence that had helped her find it. She cried out and gestured, tugging Will toward it. He stumbled, slamming into her, forcing them both to their knees.

Jess started crawling again, her sand-filled eyes streaming with tears, praying that a snarling coyote would not emerge from the ground, ready to fight for its shelter. She hesitated at the den entrance, Will's hand on her arm.

"Wait," he shouted. He began throwing handfuls of sand and gravel into the opening, trying to startle any animal already inside into showing itself. Nothing appeared. The only sound was the high-pitched roar of the wind.

An inch at a time, Will lowered himself into the den, both hands full of sharp rocks. Jess stayed far enough back so that she could get out of his way if something happened. But nothing did.

Jess waited until Will's face reappeared and he motioned for her to join him. The den was barely big enough for both of them. They sat huddled side by side, hunched over beneath the low earthen ceiling, listening to the devilish cacophony of the sandstorm.

Chapter Fourteen

Will could barely breathe. The air was thick, gritty. His makeshift mask had helped, but not nearly enough. The edges of his lips and the insides of his nostrils were caked with dust and sand. He and Jess had dug the den a little deeper in the first few hours. They rested fitfully, easing their cramped legs, their bags making lumpy pillows beneath their heads. Jess had gotten out her canteen first, sipping at the water and dampening the cloth over her nose and her cracked, swollen lips.

As the day faded into night, the wild screaming of the wind got even louder. Will lay still beside Jess, uneasy. The den was so small. He could touch the hard earth of the ceiling without straightening his arm. It was like lying in his own grave. Outside, the maddening rush of the wind went on and on, finally lulling him into a restless sleep.

Will was not sure when he had awakened from his nightmares. The wind was still roaring, but it had to be daylight outside because he could see the outline of Jess's face against the entrance. But was it dawn? Or was the sky so clouded with sand and dust that the rays of the midday sun were dimmed to a murky dusk?

Will rubbed at his eyes and instantly regretted it. The grit that clung to his lashes and eyelids scratched at his eyes painfully. He blinked rapidly until the worst of the stinging was gone. He wished desperately that he could just sleep peacefully, until the storm had ended. But his dreams had been terrifying, all about strangling, about being trapped. He stretched a little, turning slightly to lessen the pressure of the hard ground against his back. It hurt to breathe. It was impossible to stop coughing.

Will pulled his canteen out of his bag and fumbled with the cork. He drank, trying to control himself. His throat was so raw and swollen, he could barely swallow, but even the pain couldn't keep him from gulping down five mouthfuls of water when he had meant to limit himself to two.

He carefully wet the shirtsleeve that went over his nose and mouth, dabbing at his cracked lips. Abruptly, Jess woke beside him and sat up, striking her forehead against the rough ceiling. She cried out and flailed, knocking Will's canteen from his hand.

"Jess, stop it!" he tried to shout, but his voice was a grating whisper. He turned, reaching, struggling to get hold of his canteen again. He could hear the water trickling out of it, and smelled the thick, pungent odor of wet dirt.

Jess woke fully just as he managed to snatch the canteen to safety. "I'm sorry," she murmured hoarsely, then coughed. "How much spilled?"

"About half of what was left," Will told her sadly. She looked stricken. He could make out her face now. It was getting lighter. "It's all right," he rasped. "As soon as the wind drops, we can go get more."

Jess let out a long breath. "Of course. I forgot." She rose up on her elbows and got out her own canteen. She pushed the shirt away from her mouth. Will could tell she was doing exactly what he had done—trying not to drink much and gulping down the water, anyway. When she had corked her canteen and put it away, she lay back, closing her eyes.

Will flattened himself, trying to see past Jess, out the arched opening of the entrance.

Jess opened her eyes, and he saw her lips moving. He pointed at his ear, shaking his head. She repeated herself, louder this time. "What are you doing?"

"Trying to tell how high the sun is." Will propped himself up on one elbow, clearing his throat. "Can you see?"

Jess leaned down, then shook her head. "But the wind is slowing up."

Will listened. The roar had diminished. He ducked low again and stared out at the little patch of sky. It was a lot lighter now, dirty blue, not brown. He could see the whitish glare that had preceded the storm the day before. He lay back down, wondering if the sandstorm had hit the little wash where his family was camped. They would have the wagon for shelter at least—unless the wind had been strong enough to knock it over. At least Tolford would have been pinned down, too—no one could have traveled, Will was sure. He tried to rest, to still his worrisome thoughts. When the wind had dropped to a moaning whistle, he nudged Jess. "I think we could go out now."

Jess slid forward on her belly, and he could tell she was as stiff and cramped as he was. She dragged her bag up the slope and out of the den, and he followed at her heels. He watched her turn out of the wind, her makeshift mask loose. Her hair flared in the next gust as he crawled out to stand beside her.

The wind had dropped, but it was still strong. He turned away from the blowing sand as Jess had, reaching up to retie the shirtsleeves that covered his face. He was hungry and he was sure Jess was, too. He had dried meat left, but the idea of trying to eat without water made his throat tighten.

Jess was standing unsteadily, her feet wide for balance, but her shoulders were squared, and when she caught him looking at her, she raised her eyebrows. "What?"

"Cover up," he reminded her. "We have to walk upwind to get back to the spring." He loved her for not complaining. Anyone else would be whining, making things even worse. He watched Jess fuss at the shirt, pulling it down low over her eyes. She nodded when she was ready.

The wind had changed everything. The floor of the valley had been stripped of the salt that had made it shine so brilliantly in the sun. The wind had scuffed up ripple marks in the sand. As they got closer to the spring, Will could see that the tule rushes had been knocked flat by the wind.

He walked slowly through the loosened sand, sinking a few inches with each step. His thoughts felt slow again, and he struggled to think more clearly. Something was niggling at him, something he knew he should be worried about, but he couldn't remember what.

"Oh my God," Jess said, startling Will out of his reverie.

"What's wrong?"

"The wind . . . ," Jess said, pointing.

Will followed her gesture. He reeled forward, frantically trying to see the surface of the water, but he could not. He turned, walking parallel to what was left of the tules, stumbling when his right foot plunged into damp sand.

"It's buried," Jess wailed, and her voice rose over the dying wind. "The water's gone, Will!"

Will stared at what had been the water's edge.

They had fallen to their knees here and had drunk enough to get sick—then enough to live. This water had saved their lives once. It was not going to save them twice.

The wind was no more than a hard breeze now. The sky overhead was still clouded with dust, but Jess could see the disk of the sun, a copper glow in the east. She clenched and unclenched her fists, staring at the sand that obscured the little marsh. She kicked at it weakly, too tired and too hungry to do more than that. "Where's the map?" she asked hoarsely, turning toward Will.

He sat down heavily. He reached into his bag and pulled out the tin that held the map. From where she stood, Jess could see the smudges of dirt on the paper. Will spread it out, and she watched him tracing something with his finger. Then he looked up. "Maybe ten miles. Maybe fifteen."

Jess sat down. It was hard to believe that they could walk that far without food or water. She sighed, her breath painful in her dust-filled lungs. She pulled at the shirt tied around her face, suddenly irritated by it. She stuffed it into her bag. When she looked up again, Will was on his hands and knees, digging.

Puzzled, Jess watched. He was scooping out handfuls of the damp sand. It was so soft, and he could barely manage a hole big enough to fit both his hands at once before the sides began to cave in. Jess slowly figured out what he was trying to do. Why hadn't she thought of it? Her thoughts were getting muddled again.

She crawled closer to help him. Together they dug at the damp sand, the hole getting wider and wider as the sides collapsed. Breathing hard, Jess worked frantically, praying that she would soon see water seeping into the hole, forming a tiny reservoir that would fill their canteens. But the crumbling sand seemed endless, not wet enough to seep. About two feet down, they hit a layer of hard dirt.

"If we only had a shovel," Will muttered, sitting back, his breath coming in long gasps.

Jess nodded, scratching at the hard ground. She looked up suddenly. "The knife."

He stood up and went back to where they'd left their bags. She tried to find a soft spot with her fingers once more, then gave up and sat waiting. When he handed her the knife, she took it and plunged it into the soil. It sank easily enough, and she leaned forward to get a strong grip on the handle. Twisting it hard, she freed a slice of the ground and threw it to one side. Then she stabbed the knife in again, farther this time, almost up to the hilt. She leaned her weight on it, forcing the blade back and forth. Then she twisted, trying to enlarge the miniature shaft she had opened up.

Jess strained to keep her grip as she increased the pressure. A metallic snapping startled her as the knife handle suddenly came free. Losing her balance, Jess rolled to the side and lay looking at the bladeless handle, still firmly grasped in both hands. "Oh, Will, I'm sorry," she managed. Then she began to cry.

Will patted her arm awkwardly. He didn't speak, and she was glad. What was there to say? She had snapped the knife blade. It was ruined. Now, they had no other tools or weapons besides their own hands. Sobbing, she clawed at the hard dirt, tearing one fingernail, ignoring the pain and the beads of blood that rose from beneath it.

Jess felt Will tugging at her, pulling her to her feet. She fought him for a moment, trying to think of some way to at least dig out the buried blade. But how?

"Come on, Jess," Will was saying. He lifted her bag, and she took it, still looking at the slit in the ground that held the knife blade. Will put his arm over her shoulders and turned her around. He started walking. Jess stumbled along beside him.

Chapter Fifteen

Jess's legs felt wooden as she plodded along beside her brother. The wind had erased Tolford's tracks. Will accidentally located them three or four times by falling into the soft sand that had filled them. But it was impossible to see them anymore, and somewhere, after they had been walking about an hour, Jess realized that she was no longer trying—and neither was Will.

As the morning wore on, the wind fell, weakening, until it did no more than parch Jess's mouth and deepen the painful splits in her lips. They passed a dead ox, then, a mile farther on, two more. Jess's legs worked as if they were no longer a part of her, the rhythm of walking somehow overriding the pain in her blistered feet. When they rested at noon, they decided to empty their canteens. Jess felt her thoughts clear a little after drinking.

She knew that if she somehow lived through this day she would never cross a creek without stopping to drink again. Water would never be the same for her, no matter how long she lived. It was magical, heavenly. Her whole life she had complained about rainy days and waded puddles with distaste. She just hadn't known. The thought made her so sad that she felt like crying, but Will was standing up slowly, picking up his bag. He waited for her to stagger to her feet, and they began to walk again.

All afternoon, Will led the way, always heading south, lifting his head to scan the endless sand ahead of them, then dropping his eyes again. Twice he spread out the map, and they both looked at it, trying to orient themselves. It was impossible to estimate how far they had come from the buried spring. They were walking slowly, Jess knew—far more slowly than they had at first. Could Tolford be going any faster?

By early evening, Jess was fighting to resist her thirst. She had finished all but a swallow or two of her water and she was determined to save it. As badly as she wanted to drink it now, the idea of facing a whole night without even a sip was unbearable. She had seen Will drinking from his vinegar bottle earlier—was he completely out now? She was afraid to ask.

The sun was sitting on top of the mountains to the west, and the air had begun to cool off. Jess was so tired. Her legs and arms felt weighted, a burden she could barely carry. She pulled at the back of Will's shirt. He stopped and stood unsteadily, staring at her. The grayish hollows around his eyes scared her. Did she look like that, too?

"Are we . . ." She had to stop and clear her throat, then continue in a rasping whisper. "Going to rest?"

Will shook his head. "Got to keep going."

Why? Jess wanted to scream at him. She took a deep breath, intending to argue, but he was already turning away. She stood still, watching his first three or four steps, then, without meaning to, she began to follow. It was as though there was an invisible thread that tied them together. If he went on, then she had to as well.

The dusk deepened into near darkness. Then the

moon rose. Jess could hear angry thoughts in one corner of her mind. This made no sense. A clamor of coyote howls rose into the night, somewhere off to the east.

Jess looked up at the almost full moon. Its outline shimmered and danced. Will was walking slowly, his head down now, his shoulders hunched up as if he were cold.

The sand beneath their feet made a strange squeaking sound that caught Jess's attention. She tipped her head, wondering if it had been there all along, or if it had just begun. She looked past Will, toward the moonlit peaks on their right. Even if they walked all night, they weren't going to gain much ground, she heard herself thinking. They were walking too slowly, their steps ragged and uneven.

Jess fell to her knees. It didn't hurt and she giggled, or tried to, but the pain in her throat was sudden and intense. By the time she looked up again, Will was a shadowy form, receding into the darkness ahead of her.

Lurching to her feet, Jess concentrated fiercely on every step, willing herself to stay upright. She tried to call out Will's name, but her voice was gone, her breath rushing out of her mouth without making any sound at all. He walked on, his head low, his silhouette a shambling ghost in the moonlight.

Jess quickened her steps, stiff-legged and clumsy. She wanted to tell him about her two last swallows of water. That would make him stop, would persuade him that they should rest for a while. She stumbled, leaning forward to grab the back of his shirt. He turned, and she could see a deep scowl on his haggard face. She tried to explain and was frightened by the croaking sound she heard herself make. The ground suddenly seemed uneven, unstable.

Turning away, covering her mouth with one hand, she staggered beneath the weight of her own fear. She tried to stay on her feet, tried to keep the swirling dizziness from consuming her. Above her head stars glittered in the sky. The moon was yellowish now, well above the horizon. Then, at ground level, a distant reddish light caught her eye and she faced it, her thoughts slow and blurred.

Jess blinked, not believing it at first. She reached out blindly to Will, afraid that if she looked away, even for a second, the reddish twinkle would disappear. "Will." This time she managed to whisper, and he somehow heard her because he appeared at her shoulder, his face as angular as a skull's in the moonlight. She pointed, and he said the words she had been too frightened to say: "Tolford's fire."

Will did not remember walking the last few miles. Mr. Tolford had explained how they had almost gotten shot by not responding to his shouts to declare themselves. Will didn't remember that, either. For him, life had begun again in the back of one of Tolford's wagons, shaded from the sun by the dusty canvas, Jess lying unconscious on a pallet of blankets beside his own.

The first day had been the worst. His headache had been like a hammer beating at his forehead. Jess had vomited most of the day, spewing up the fresh water Moses had carried from the spring. Mr. Tolford's gruff demeanor had softened under his amazement that they had managed to find him. Moses had turned out to be a good sick-nurse with a quiet voice and gentle patience. Jess had been embarrassed to have him clean her up, but had been too weak to do anything but sob.

Now, on the fourth morning, Jess was still sleeping.

She had awakened twice in the night to ask if Tolford had returned with Ma and Pa yet. Will kept explaining that it would be two more days, or three, before Tolford got back. Jess reacted with quiet courage every time. Then her dreams would make her forget what she already knew, and she would ask again.

For the first time, Will felt like getting up. He waited until he heard Moses whistling. Then he got to his feet and carefully stepped down out of the wagon, leaning against the gate until he felt steady enough to walk a few steps.

"Want something to keep busy at?" Moses asked, looking up from his fire tending.

Will nodded, realizing that was exactly what he needed. "I still feel weak as a kitten, though."

Moses grinned at him. "You can pick rocks out of tonight's beans, can't you?"

Will nodded and went to sit on one of the overturned cheese crates near the fire pit. Moses brought him a cracker box, lined with a dirty flannel cloth. Will spilled the beans slowly into the box. He carefully rolled them back and forth with his hand, picking out the tiny stones that could break a tooth.

"What's that?" Moses said quietly. Will glanced

up at him. Moses jutted out his chin, gesturing. "Somebody coming?"

Will looked up the valley and saw a plume of dust in the distance. He sat, transfixed, as it came closer, trailing out behind whatever was raising it. Another few minutes revealed the shape of a team of mules pulling a wagon. Four oxen were strung out behind it, linked by a lead rope. Will stood up, carefully setting down the box that held the beans. He took four or five steps toward the coming wagon, then spun around and broke into a heavy-footed run. He had to tell Jess.

"Are they here?" she asked again as he woke her.

"Maybe," Will said. "But Jess, we don't know if Pa made it or if . . ." He trailed off when he saw the dark sorrow that passed through her eyes. He helped her get up and steadied her as she got down from the wagon.

Will could see Mr. Tolford on the bench now, unmistakable in his high-crowned hat. Beside him, clearer with every second that passed, was a woman wearing an apron. Ma was all right! To her left was a form too confusing to name. Will stared, the sun's glare forcing him to shade his eyes.

"It's the boys," Jess whispered roughly, then paused. "Jed's standing in the wagon bed behind Eli."

As soon as she said it, the weird silhouette made sense to Will and he felt a smile dragging at his cracked lips. They looked like they were all right. But where was Pa?

The wagon rolled into camp, and Will and Jess moved forward together as Ma came down from the wagon bench. She touched Jess's sunburned face, then embraced them both. She stood back after a few seconds, dabbing at her eyes, sniffling. Will hesitated, glancing at the wagon, afraid. . . .

"Thank God you're safe!"

Will closed his eyes in relief at the sound of his father's voice. He freed himself from his mother and saw Pa coming toward him, leaning hard on a walking stick. His face was gaunt and pinched, but the pallor was gone from his skin and there was no new staining on his trousers.

"I'm proud of how you took care of your sister, son."

"Jess is the one who kept me going, Pa," Will said, ducking his head at his father's praise. Eli and Jed were scrambling down, their sunburned faces tired but happy as they ran to Jess.

"Tolford says we can travel with him," Pa said quietly. "He says there can't be but five days or a week before we're out of this valley."

Will looked up to see Mr. Tolford watching him. "We brought your water barrels, and the four oxen still fit to walk," he explained. "But we'll all make it out, son." He pushed his hat back, then turned to unhitch the mules.

"I have never been so glad to see anyone in my life," Pa said, looking at Will. "I am so proud of you both. And grateful."

"Your leg is better?" Jess asked him.

He nodded. "Fever's gone, and it hurts a lot less."

Ma began to weep again. Will looked up at the sky. It had turned out all right. They were going to live. They were going to make it to the gold fields. He looked at Jess and saw her try to smile, touching her swollen lips with one finger.

"We made it, Will."

He nodded. No one else would ever understand what those words meant, he realized. Not Pa or Ma, or the boys or anyone else he ever told the story to. No one but his brave sister. He put his arm around her shoulders, and they led their family into camp.

Turn the page for more
survival stories in:

Gavin Reilly stood on the boat deck of the *Titanic*, his eyes closed tightly. He gripped the handrail and counted to ten. Then he opened his eyes again. He had to get over this. He *had* to get used to looking out over the open water. After a few dizzying seconds, he turned landward, gulping huge breaths of the cool air. He stared at the coastline and the green hills above Queenstown, Ireland. This was ridiculous. He had been swimming since he was a baby. He had never been afraid of water in his life.

"Are you all right?"

Gavin looked up to see a girl with light brown hair, and a scattering of freckles across the bridge of her nose. She looked concerned. Her accent, broadly American, sounded brash and rude.

"Are you sick?"

Gavin shook his head. There was no way to explain what was wrong with him. He didn't really understand it himself. "I'm fine," he said, staring back at the shoreline.

The town's docks were all too small for the *Titanic*, so the enormous liner had been anchored two miles offshore. Passengers, goods, and mailbags were being brought out to her. Gavin watched the tenders and bumboats scuttling back and forth. The *Ireland* was not a small boat, but it looked like a toy beside the *Titanic*. The *America* stood off a little distance, waiting its turn to unload.

Gavin watched a bumboat come alongside. Most of them were loaded with Irish goods. The first-class nabobs and their finely dressed wives would have their chance to buy Irish linen and lace, even if they couldn't go ashore.

Gavin glanced sideways. The girl was still standing nearby, but she was looking out to sea now, her hair blowing in the wind. Gavin wanted more than anything to turn and face the open water, but he knew he couldn't. He moved a little ways away from the girl, hoping she wouldn't follow.

Gavin leaned against the metal railing. The familiar green curve of the south Irish coast was less than two miles away over the water. He stared at Queenstown with its narrow streets and closely packed buildings. He sighed.

The hills behind the town were so green, they reminded him of his home outside Belfast. He could imagine his brothers and sisters tending the potato patch in the high pasture. Sean's voice would be ringing out over little Katie's giggles. Gavin could almost see her, freckled and pink-faced. Liam would be arguing with Mary. The little ones would be with Mother at home, lined up on her cot for noontime nap. Gavin felt the now-familiar physical ache that always accompanied thoughts of his family. He might never see them again.

"Are you ill?" the girl asked.

Gavin glanced at her and shook his head, then pointedly turned his back. He forced himself to look out to sea. The cold gray water stretched all the way to the horizon. He wasn't sure why it bothered him so much. Everyone agreed the *Titanic* was unsink-able. That very morning they had run a full dress rehearsal emergency; alarms sounding, they had closed all the watertight doors.

Gavin had been so determined to get a position on the *Titanic* that he had traveled to Southampton, lied about his age, and stood in line with several hundred others to be interviewed. Conor's letters from New York had set him dreaming of a different life. Like all older brothers, Conor wanted him to have opportu-nities, too. Their mother had lit a candle for Conor the day he had sailed for America. Now she would light two every Sunday. The idea of the candles made Gavin feel a sharp stab of homesickness.

"I didn't mean to intrude," the girl said apologet-ically. He glanced at her, about to apologize for his own rudeness, but she had already turned away.

He watched her walk past the gigantic funnel that jutted up at an angle from the deck. The other three were real and spouted black smoke when the *Titanic* was underway. This one was fake, nothing more than a huge air vent. Still, like the others, it was anchored with thick steel cables. Gavin saw the girl start down the steep stairs toward the third-class promenade.

"Hey, Gavin! You'd better get back down to the galley." Lionel's voice startled him. The tall, blond-haired boy dropped onto one of the wooden benches along the handrail. "Mr. Hughes will see you slacking, and they'll be booting you off. That would shame your roommates, you know."

Gavin grinned. "I would hate to do that."

"Well, Harry and I would be shamed at any rate. I'm not sure Wallace has it in him."

They both laughed. "I've only been up here a few minutes," Gavin said. "I needed fresh air."

Lionel shrugged. "Are you seasick? At anchor? It's going to be like sailing a whole city across the Atlantic, Gavin. She barely rolls at all."

Gavin shot one more glance at the open water and felt his stomach tighten. "I'd better get started washing the new potatoes. First class is going to have them boiled *parmentier*."

"Work hard and you can end up a first-class steward like me." Lionel stood up straight, clowning, squaring his shoulders in exaggerated pride. "I have to go down to the dining room to deliver a message."

"I'll go down with you," Gavin said, getting to his feet.

Together they headed toward the second-class entrance. Gavin reached out to open the door. Side by side they started down the long stairway. Their steps were timed to a rhythmic patter that kept them moving downward at almost a running pace. Lionel had taught Gavin how to run the stairs like this and he shot him a grin of approval. "You're getting good."

Gavin grinned back, feeling better.

As they descended past the windows of the Palm Court, he saw the first-class passengers seated in the elaborately decorated garden room. There were a few men onboard who were so wealthy, their clothing had probably cost more than it took to feed Gavin's family for a whole year. He had seen one woman wearing a necklace of diamonds so big, they shot glitters across the room.

On the B-deck landing, Gavin could smell the heavy scent of tobacco coming from the second-class smoking room. Lionel lifted one hand to cover his nose and mouth. Gavin nodded. First-class was the worst—expensive cigars had a pungent odor that clung to the very walls.

As they went deeper into the ship, Gavin felt his nervousness subside a little. Down here, the *Titanic* was much like a grand hotel. It was easier to forget the deep gray water that would soon separate him from his family and from the farm where he had lived his whole life.

"What time are you off Saturday night?" Lionel asked.

Gavin grabbed the handrail as they rounded the landing on C-deck. "After cleanup. Around ten."

"Come up to the first-class dining room—it's empty by then, and a few of us are going to have a card game."

Gavin glanced at the side of Lionel's face, then looked back at the stairs. "I've been coming up here." He pointed at the second-class library as they started downward again.

"You're going to read? When you could be playing poker?"

Gavin smiled and nodded. "I have to get to New York with all my pay. I can't expect my brother to support me."

Lionel slowed as they reached D-deck. "Come up if you change your mind. You can just sit with us; you don't have to play."

"I will, thanks."

Gavin watched as Lionel went into the first-class

dining saloon. Through the open door Gavin saw that the room was still pretty full. The stewards were just beginning to clear away dirty dishes. Lionel's rakish grin disappeared, and his face became a mask of politeness as he turned and bent to whisper discreetly to a woman in a green silk gown.

Gavin shook his head as he pulled the door closed and turned to cross the landing. Going into the first-class pantry, he walked fast, rounding the corner by the neatly stacked crates of Waken & McLaughlin wine. The roast cook and one of the confectioners came through the galley door ahead of him. He stopped and turned sideways to let them pass. Neither man acknowledged his presence.

Gavin watched them walk away. He wasn't like Lionel. It was hard for him to smile at people who were rude to him, whether they were crew or passengers. He hurried into the galley, wishing he had been hired on as a dining room steward. They had it easier. A half hour after the last passenger left the dining saloons, the stewards would be changing the white tablecloths and setting the tables for the next meal. Then they would have a break.

"Hey! Gavin!"

Gavin turned to see Harry making his way across the crowded galley. His sharp-featured face was smudged with flour. He was already developing the short-strided, agile walk necessary to avoid collisions in the crowded, busy room.

Cooking never ceased here, except for a few hours in the middle of the night. The bakers began at three in the morning. The cooks started preparing breakfast early, then began lunch before the breakfast dishes were cleared. Dinner preparation sometimes started a day in advance, all the meals overlapping—only the chefs understood the schedule.

"Where have you been off to?" Harry asked, dodging a pantryman carrying an enormous, bloody roast. "You missed a chance to watch the pastry chef make éclairs."

Gavin shrugged. Harry wanted to be a chef someday and he rarely left the galley. "I went up for air," Gavin told him. "I just like to see the sky once in a while."

Harry nodded vaguely, turning when the sauce chef bellowed out an order. Then his eyes focused on Gavin again. "What do you have to do now?"

Gavin made a face. "Wash a hundred and twenty

pounds of new potatoes." Harry laughed, and Gavin pretended to take a swing at him. "It isn't funny. I hate the new potatoes worst of all. I can't even use the wire brushes because the skins tear so easily."

Harry grinned over his shoulder as he walked away. "Better you than me."

Gavin went to his basin. The pantrymen had already brought in the bags. He stared at the lettering. Whoever Charles Papas was, he sure raised a lot of potatoes.

"When do we raise anchor?" someone yelled behind him.

"Soon," the answer came. "Less than half an hour."

Gavin's throat tightened. There was no turning back now.